SCOT ON HER TRAIL

CAROLINE LEE

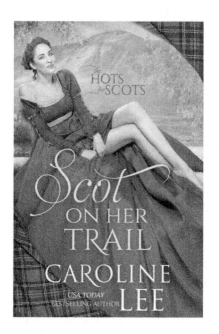

Duncan Oliphant's father has insisted he—and all of his brothers—marry and start producing grandsons...like, *yesterday*. And Dunc is having none of it.

All he wants in life is a small cottage behind his forge and enough gold and silver to craft valuable delicate jewelry.

But he *is* the laird's son, albeit illegitimate, and he knows he has a duty to do; one he's happy to postpone, as he takes one more commission, which has him traveling across the Highlands, gold in hand.

Which is, of course, the worst time to be attacked by highwaymen.

Even worse if it's not a *man* at all, but a highway*woman*—a gorgeous, feisty one he accidentally kissed a fortnight ago at his brother's wedding.

What in the world is Skye Duncan doing, robbing unsuspecting travelers?

The only way to discover the truth—and get back his gold—is to kidnap the highwaywoman and offer a trade.

Aye, this will go swimmingly…until it doesn't.

Skye clearly isn't a meek and delicate lady. And despite their rocky beginning, she simply can't ignore the way Duncan's kisses made her feel, or how his offered solution might just be what she needs to hang up her sword for good.

Can a goldsmith who only wants a simple life make peace with a determined highwaywoman, for the sake of their clans' futures?

Or is the gulf between them—and their own personal history—just too much for them to overcome?

And whatever *did* happen to all that gold?

Pick up the second book in the riotously funny *The Hots for Scots* series and get ready for a rollicking good time!

OTHER BOOKS BY CAROLINE LEE

Want the scoop on new books? Join Caroline's Cohort, an exclusive reader group! Or sign up for my mailing list by texting "Caroline" to 42828 to get started!

Steamy Scottish Historicals:
The Sinclair Jewels (4 books)
The Highland Angels (4 books)
The Hots for Scots (7 books)

Sensual Historical Westerns:
Black Aces (3 books)
Sunset Valley (3 books)
Everland Ever After (10 books)
The Sweet Cheyenne Quartet (6 books)

Sweet Contemporary Westerns
Quinn Valley Ranch (5 books)
River's End Ranch (14 books)
The Cowboys of Cauldron Valley (3+ books)

Click **here** to find a complete list of Caroline's books.

*Sign up for Caroline's Newsletter to receive exclusive content and freebies, as well as first dibs on her books! Or if newsletters aren't your thing, follow her on **Bookbub** for a quick, concise new release alert every time she publishes a book!*

CHAPTER 1

THERE WAS SAFETY IN NUMBERS.

At least, that's what Duncan Oliphant told himself, as he wondered, yet again, *why* he'd chosen to ride alongside a mute monk. The monk—not much older than Duncan himself—had obviously taken a vow of silence, bless his good intentions.

But it made him boring as hell for a companion though.

Duncan was used to being the silent one in the group. His brothers—all five of them—were more loquacious than he, and most of them were better tempered as well. But for the first time in his life, he was finding it damned annoying to have to be the one to carry on a conversation.

"Are ye headed to Fearn, then?" When the monk glanced at him, one brow raised in question, Duncan shrugged. "I ken ye left Eriboll the same time I did, and we've been riding together for almost two days. Since there's nae other abbeys near, I assume ye're traveling to Fearn?"

After a moment's hesitation, the monk—who'd kept his hood pulled up far enough to almost cover his bushy orange brows—nodded quickly, then turned back to the road.

Duncan stifled his sigh.

Safety in numbers.

Hoarse Harold, the notorious—and sometimes deadly—highway-man, was rumored to be working in these parts lately.

No' that a mute monk will make much of a difference if we're attacked by brigands.

For that matter, Duncan might not either. His sword hung at his hip, and though his shoulders were broad from swinging a smith's hammers, he was no warrior. He'd trained with his brothers, well enough, and he knew which end of the blade to stick into the other guy...but he much preferred to *create*, than destroy.

Which explained why his pouch was so full, and why he was so concerned about highwaymen on this particular journey.

Unconsciously, his free hand dropped to the pouch, adjusting its heavy weight to lie more comfortably against his thigh. The gold in it made it heavy, but he refused to remove it from his belt. Who knew what might happen to a man's purse at the inns he'd be staying in?

Settling himself in the saddle once more, he caught the monk's glance toward the purse. The other man quickly looked away, but not before Duncan saw the question in his eyes.

Too bad, friend.

Dunc might not be the most talkative of men, but by St. Simon's kneecap, he wasn't going to go around bragging about his burden.

Before he could think of something else to bring up—something to distract the too-curious monk, a wagon rumbled over the hill ahead of them. Both Duncan and the monk moved their mounts over to the side of the path to let the wagon pass.

The wagon was driven by an older man, a crofter by the look of the wool pallets in the rear, and two lasses who must be his daughters sat behind him. Both of them giggled to one another and waved cheekily to the two men as they passed.

The monk peered intently at the wagon, as if there were some-thing fascinating about the wool, but Duncan decided he was likely looking at the lasses.

When they continued on their journey after the wagon went by, Duncan hummed thoughtfully. "I am no' married. But if I had to be, I always thought I'd choose a lass like that, ye ken? A woman of the earth and soil."

A woman like his mam.

A woman naught like Skye MacIan.

The monk was watching him, and Duncan could sense the question in his gaze.

"I'm one of six sons, aye? All of us bastards, and all of us the same age." Three sets of twins, all born the same year to a Highland laird, who was sowing his wild oats a little too vigorously. "Da says we're all to marry this year and start presenting him with grandbairns. The first one to give him a legitimate grandson will— Och, it doesnae matter."

The first one to present Da with a legitimate grandson would become the next Laird Oliphant, a duty Duncan wanted about as much as another hole in his head. Two ears, two nostrils, and a mouth were enough to keep up with, *thankyeverramuch*. Imagine having to handle the shite of an entire *clan*!

Nay, let Alistair—who'd been handling most of the Oliphant's shite now for years anyhow—or even Duncan's twin, Finn, become the next laird. Finn was far more charming and had just married his "true love," Lady Fiona MacIan. He was far ahead of them all when it came to Da's dictates.

I'll likely be an uncle by spring. As long as the lad doesnae call me Uncle Dunc, we'll be fine.

Still musing the whole thing over, Duncan grunted. " 'Tisnae as if I never intend to marry. I just dinnae want to do it on Da's orders, ye ken? Oh, dinnae give me that look," he snapped at the monk. "I ken plenty of men marry on their father's orders. But..." He shrugged. "I am nae one special. Just a smith."

I dinnae want to be a laird.

Was it his imagination, or did the monk roll his eyes a bit before he turned his attention back to the road when he announced his profession?

But Duncan was still thinking about Da's directive. He'd thought of little else for the last fortnight, really.

Shifting uneasily in the saddle, he cleared his throat. "The problem is, while I might've thought I had a wife picked out—or a *type* of wife at least—" Cutting himself off, he shook his head as he realized he had no idea how to finish his sentence. "The problem is, I met someone...*else*."

Skye MacIan, his twin brother's new wife's twin sister. A convoluted relationship for an incredibly simple attraction.

Attraction?

Nay. What he'd felt for Skye went *far* beyond mere attraction.

As soon as he'd seen her—combing down her horse in the Oliphant stables as he prepared to leave for Lairg—he'd been enthralled by her. Not necessarily by her beauty, although she was bonny enough.

But it was her certainty, her confidence, her *complete* confidence, which had reached under his kilt and tugged hard at his cock.

And he hadn't been the same since, especially since the moment he'd *kissed* her.

Of course, the second time he'd kissed her, she'd punched him.

They'd worked that out—a case of mistaken identity, which was likely Finn's fault, the horse's arse—and now were technically related by marriage. But that hadn't wiped the slate clean as far as Duncan and Skye were concerned.

He'd humiliated her, and she'd punched him.

And had she threatened to kill him at their sibling's wedding celebration?

He was still unclear on that.

His thoughts were miles away, on a certain Scottish spitfire, so the fork in the road ahead of him caught him by surprise.

When the monk dragged his horse's head—and 'twas quite a fine mount, for a simple monk!—to the south, Duncan realized this must be the turn-off for the monastery.

Knowing the man wouldn't answer him, nonetheless, Duncan lifted his hand in farewell. "Safe travels, friend. My thanks for listening to my problems."

The monk's response was a surprised scowl, then a quick nod, before kicking his horse into a trot.

Duncan shrugged and turned his attention to the easterly route. The Oliphant lands—*home*—lay in that direction. And now he was alone.

Alone with his thoughts.

And his gold.

His fingers curled unwillingly around his sword hilt.

The monk had been poor company, but at least there had been safety in numbers.

———

"THINK ye we should recruit another man?"

"Nay, the split is poor enough between the five of us."

" 'Twould be better, if we didnae send so much to the laird—"

"Quiet, lad. A honied cake like *ye* dinnae ken what 'tis like to lead a clan."

Skye MacIan—daughter of a laird, sister of another one—pretended great interest in the knobby stick she was whittling while her men argued. It wasn't so much an *argument*, as a discussion they tended to have whenever there wasn't enough prey to keep them occupied.

"What say ye, Bean? Do ye *like* sending half of what we take to the castle, while we content ourselves with a pittance?"

Young Rabbie always voiced these complaints. Skye wasn't sure taking him on had been the best idea, but his uncle had vouched for him, and she trusted Fergus's judgement. Still, the greedy whining could get a mite annoying.

A mite? She snorted softly. *More like Rabbie is a* heap *of annoyances.*

Bean, their giant, stood with his arms crossed and legs planted. The dear, dense man was a champion when it came to standing still. No one could do *nothing* quite as well as he. Now, he frowned, and opened his mouth in that way he had, which indicated he'd be uttering something deep and profound any day now.

"Aye."

Ah, there 'tis.

Skye tucked her chin against her chest and hid her smile as she worked her bollock dagger around a particularly gnarled knot in the stick.

"Aye, what?" Rabbie whined.

"Aye, I like sending half of what we take to the castle. Laird MacIan needs it."

"See?" Fergus jumped on Bean's words, scowling at his nephew. "We all understand, 'tis our tarting duty to the whole fruitcaking clan. The MacIan relies on us, even if he dinnae ken it."

"Well, 'tis why I think we dinnae need another member of our band," Rabbie grumbled, lounging against a boulder near the stream. "The pickings are poor enough. And me mam can only—"

"Yer *mam?*" Fergus pushed himself to his feet and began to pace, likely to keep from smacking the lad on the back of his head. "Yer puir, custardy mam never sees a piece of our prizes, I'll wager. The way ye spend it all at the tavern when ye think we cannae see— *Och, honey!*"

Well, if the real cursing was starting, that was Skye's cue to interrupt.

"Enough," she said quietly, certain in the knowledge her men would listen and respect her words. She pointed the phallic stick at Rabbie's nose. "Ye are riling yer uncle up, which will do none of us any good."

The lad had the grace to appear abashed, but Skye was never sure if it was because he respected her...or her position as *Lady.*

So her frown was a little fiercer when she continued, "This is the way things have to be. I trust nae one else when it comes to keeping our clan afloat, and sometimes I wonder about my choices as is."

From Bean came a low rumble she recognized as his chuckle, but she held Rabbie's gaze until the boy nodded and dropped his chin in acknowledgement.

"Aye, milady. Sorry, Uncle."

"*Fig tart,*" Fergus mumbled, and Skye sighed.

The older man really was wonderfully supportive. He'd been the MacIan farrier when Skye was a girl, but now his son had that role. She'd more or less adopted Fergus, and when she'd turned high-wayman—*highwaywoman?*—Fergus had been the first she'd approached with her scheme.

He'd always stood beside her, even when he shouldn't.

One of those times had been when he'd caught her repeating a curse word he'd said was strong enough to make a lassie's hair curl. Skye, at age ten, had pointed out her brown hair *did* curl, so he shouldn't worry.

Still, the dear man hadn't wanted to offend her, and had refused to add to her corruption. So he'd learned to yell *other* things. *Sweeter* things, or so he claimed.

Like *honey* and *fig tart*.

And he did it for her.

If that wasn't love, Skye wasn't sure what was.

Smiling now, she pushed herself to her feet, brushing the shavings from her fine crimson gown as she did so. She slid her dagger into the sheath at her waist, making sure it hung against the back of her thigh, and thus, was less obvious.

After all, she might *look* like a lady in this gown, but there was no reason to let their prey know she was aught else...until it was too late.

She swept the stick around the clearing. "Do ye ken what this is?"

Fergus actually flushed, which caused Skye to frown. Rabbie snickered, and Bean shrugged.

"I dunno, but is it ribbed for yer pleasure?"

Sucking in a startled gasp, Skye glanced down at the stick she'd been absent-mindedly whittling.

Oh.

Oh, it *did* look a bit like a—

With a frustrated grunt, she tossed the thing into the woods and resisted the urge to wipe her palm on her gown. "I *meant* this...this bickering," she snapped, with a roll of her eyes. " 'Tis naught more than *boredom*."

Taking a deep breath, she crossed her arms in front of her chest and glared at Rabbie, who was still snickering. "If ye dinnae like this arrangement, ye are welcome to find *other* gainful employment. I've made things simple for us, I think. Away from our homes only once a month or so, and enough prizes to line yer purses in between. Do ye no' agree?"

With a sigh and a great roll of his eyes, Rabbie finally agreed. "Aye, milady. 'Tis a fine arrangement. I just wish—"

"That my sister-in-law had no' drained our coffers dry? That she dinnae care so much for frivolity and finery and *stupidity*, that she thinks naught of spending my brother's—and my clan's—gold?" Mayhap there was a *bit* of bitterness seeping into Skye's voice. "Aye, I wish those things too."

"Lassie," Fergus murmured quietly, " 'tis no' yer fault the Lady Allison does those things."

"Nay, 'tis no'," she agreed, then dropped her head back to stare up at the sky through the reaching branches of the oak they stood under. "But 'tis up to me to do something about it."

"Why?"

Bean's question was unexpected. The big man tended to only do what he was told to do, and not worry about the rest.

"Because," she said gently, "I am the last MacIan left at home besides Stewart. My brother is the laird, and he loves that shrew of a wife for some reason." Likely because she was about to present him with the long-awaited MacIan heir. "My sisters have all married, and my brothers are gone as well." Two had joined the church, and one had died in a stupid border skirmish. " 'Tis up to *me* to ensure the MacIans have enough gold to last through next winter."

Especially now since Fiona had married and moved to Oliphant land.

It had only been a sennight since Skye had returned from Oliphant Castle, her sister's new home, and *Blessed Virgin*, but she missed Fiona! Her twin was so in love, it was sickening, but Skye had to smile at the thought of Fee's stomach swelling with child.

Any day now, judging how often I had to find someplace else to sleep while Finn snuck into our room.

Her relationship with her brother-in-law might've started out rocky, but it had improved *slightly* when she'd learned Finn Oliphant wasn't the philandering rake she'd assumed.

Nay, that hadn't been *Finn* she'd kissed in the stable; hadn't been *Finn* who'd woken her from a sound sleep with his lips and hands—his rough, glorious hands!—on her body. And it hadn't been *Finn* she'd punched.

It hadn't been *Finn* who'd woken such a yearning *need* inside her.

Nay, it had been his identical twin brother, Duncan, each time.

Duncan Oliphant. One of the laird's six bastard sons. The one who wanted so little to do with her, he'd left his own home right after his twin's wedding, rather than risk having to be polite to her.

At the celebration, she'd brought him ale because he'd looked lonely…and he'd asked her if it was poisoned.

With a slight snort, she remembered her response.

If I wanted to kill ye, Dunc, I'd do it with a blade.

She remembered the surprise—and dare she hope, *respect*, which had flashed in his eyes then.

And she'd spent a fortnight trying to forget it.

"Lassie…?"

Fergus's quiet prompt pulled her from her memories. She raised a brow in his direction, and he flushed again, but didn't back down.

"When will ye be finished?"

"With thieving?"

He nodded, then stopped his pacing to stand beside Bean. "When will enough be enough? I ken ye are careful to pick only those who can afford our *taxes*. And by yer orders, we dinnae prey on women or bairns. Yer honor is all that's standing between us and an eternity in custarding Hell."

"Her *rules* are all that's standing between us and riches," Rabbie muttered.

"*Sweet berries!*"

Stifling her sigh, Skye planted her fists on her hips. "If ye provoke yer uncle again, laddie, ye'll feel the back of my hand." Although she was only two years Rabbie's senior, she lifted her chin and held his gaze until he looked away.

"I'm just short because Hoarse Harold has taken our best pickings," he muttered.

She narrowed her eyes at the lad's weak apology.

Unfortunately, it was true. They'd *all* been on edge since the beginning of the summer, when another band of footpads had moved into the area.

Excuse me? We're no' footpads. We're highwaymen. *Women. Whatever.*

Skye might've had too much honor for a highwaywoman, but Hoarse Harold made up for that. He robbed from rich and poor alike, and she'd even heard rumors of *murders*. With him in the area—and far too close to MacIan land—Skye was becoming nervous about taking her men out at all.

'Twas only a matter of time before the outrage at Hoarse Harold's actions became so loud, the Crown was called in to help, and where would Skye and her band—and the MacIan clan—be then?

Mayhap Fergus's plan to quit is a smart one.

Still, she couldn't allow her men to see her hesitation. So, frowning, she turned back to Fergus.

"And what does my *honor* have to do with quitting?"

Fergus exchanged glances with Bean, and the bigger man dropped his hand to the hilt of his sword. Everyone there knew he would never draw it, but it made him happy to have the scabbard at his side.

When Bean just shrugged, Fergus swallowed, then turned back to her. "Ye're a *lady*, Skye." Before she could scoff, he hurried on. "Dinnae deny it, lass. Ye're a *lady*, with expectations."

"Stitching and tapestries—"

"Marriage and alliances," the older man gently corrected.

Desperate to hide the way her mind had immediately jumped back to the memory of Duncan Oliphant's lips on hers, Skye's scowl darkened.

That didn't deter her old friend though.

"Even if ye never marry, Skye, the fate of the MacIan clan is *no'* on yer shoulders. If that berries-and-cream brother of yers would just stand up to his wife, and tell the woman to quit bleeding us dry, mayhap—"

With a sigh, she interrupted him. "Stewart doesnae ken—or doesnae *want* to see—what Allison is doing to us."

"Then *make him*." Fergus stepped forward, his hands stretched out toward her. "Make him understand, so he can put a stop to this, and so ye can quit putting yer life in danger just for some coin."

"She could always marry some rich laird," Rabbie pointed out unhelpfully, "and get the coin that way."

Fergus reacted before she could, stepping toward his disrespectful nephew with a raised hand.

She *might've* stopped him, although the Blessed Virgin knew the lad needed a good slap, had the sound of hooves not interrupted them before she could.

"Pierre!" Rabbie cried, sounding relieved.

The Frenchman was the last member of their band, and it had been his turn on watch duty. The boring job consisted of hiding in the cover of the woods along the road, about a mile north. When a likely mark passed, he would run for his horse and take a short-cut back to where the rest of them waited.

Skye's attention immediately went to their fifth member as he galloped into their little clearing. Pierre had been a good judge of prey since he'd come into their band, and although the communication was difficult, she trusted him.

And she trusted that pleased grin on his face.

A new mark.

She sent an excited smile to Fergus. "Looks like today willnae be the day to quit, auld man."

And he was grinning too. "What did ye see, Pierre?"

Hurriedly, the Frenchman—who was a few years older than Skye, with a thick mustache—slid from his horse and gestured excitedly toward the main road. "*J'adore le pamplemousse!*"

Fergus, Skye, and Rabbie all turned to Bean. He might be a slow thinker, but he was the only one of them who spoke French.

"What'd he say?" Rabbie asked, already fingering his sword hilt.

"Pierre says there's a man coming, wearing a sword."

"Sword means he kens how to use it," Fergus muttered.

"Sword means he has something to protect," Rabbie countered.

Skye had to admit the lad was right. "He's all alone, Pierre? Ye think he's carrying something worthwhile?"

"*Où est la bibliothèque?*"

Without being asked, Bean translated. "He looks worthy."

Looking from Pierre to Rabbie's excited expressions, Skye made up her mind. Fergus might be ready for her to quit, but she had a duty to her clan.

This traveler was an easy mark and might have enough coin to enable them all to head home.

Her mind made up, Skye reached for her braid and began untying it. "We'll use the usual distraction, lads." Fingers flying, she met each of her men's eyes, certain they knew their roles. "Let us make some coin!"

"*Mon aéroglisseur est plein d'anguilles!*"

"Aye!" Rabbie cried, as Bean grunted.

But Fergus just shook his head. "*Fig tart!*"

CHAPTER 2

Duncan had to admit, it *was* a beautiful day, and a man couldn't be on his guard *all* the time, no matter what he held in his purse.

And home was only a few hours away.

A sennight ago, he wouldn't have been so anxious to return home —in fact, he'd lingered in Eriboll much longer than necessary to ensure the MacIan contingent had enough time to leave Oliphant lands before he returned. Of course, with Fiona there, he'd be struck by memories of Skye every time he looked at her identical—

Shut up.

Aye, it was a lovely day, and there was no need for mucking it up by thinking about his shame.

Tilting his head back to the sun, Duncan forced his mind on something else.

Anything else.

A bawdy song, mayhap?

"'Twas springtime when I met her, in the merry month of May.
I was camping by the roadside, to escape the heat of the day.
She was passing by my campfire, and she sent me an admiring look.
She seemed a lass who'd like a pass, one I could stand to fook."

His brother Kiergan, in particular, liked to tease him about his singing, but Duncan didn't mind. He knew his mind worked differently than others, and he could easily see art and beauty where his brothers didn't.

'Twas what made his jewelry designs so sought-after, now that Master Claire was older.

His lips curled up as he reached the chorus.

"So, *buck-a-diddle-diddle, buck-a-dilly-ay, buck-a-diddle-diddle, I kenned I had to lie!*

Help, oh help, oh help me lass, I'm in need of yer gentle touch,

I've injured myself, I need yer love, 'twillnae take too much!

'Tis my cock, ye see, tis grown so big, I cannae even piss,

Only one thing to do to help me through is give it a little kiss!"

Halfway through that verse, he thought he'd heard hoofbeats, but pausing, decided he was wrong. The road was hilly here, and 'twas possible for another rider to be coming toward him without him seeing. So Duncan shrugged, settled himself easier in the saddle, and continued south.

Toward home.

"*Oh, buck-a-diddle-diddle, buck-a-dilly-ay—*"

When he spied the flash of crimson in the hedge by the side of the road, he slowed his horse. Frowning, he glanced about.

The road was bordered by a copse of fir trees on one side, and brambles on the other. No reason for there to be anything *crimson* out here.

Not seeing any danger, he cautiously edged his horse closer.

There, in the ditch beside the road…

Why was there *silk* piled there?

And…was that a hand? A *woman's* hand?

Before his mind could really process what he was seeing, Duncan was out of his saddle, sprinting for the flash of red silk.

Aye, *'twas* a woman!

Dropping to his knees beside her, Duncan realized his hands were curled into fists. *St. Simon's hairy bollocks*, but he felt useless! He forced himself to breathe as he studied her.

She was lying on her side, curled up as if in pain. Her brown hair

—such luscious curls—fell freely around her face and shoulders, before being ground into the dirt beneath her.

What had happened?

He forced his hands to open, to reach gently for her. His fingertips skimmed her arm, her shoulder, as gently as he handled his gold and silver. She made no sound or movement, and he couldn't tell if anything was broken.

There was no blood though, which he decided was a good sign.

Where in damnation was her horse?

Duncan dragged his gaze away from her to scan the road and the trees once more. *Naught.* And she was still just as unmoving.

He needed to turn her over to check for injuries he couldn't see.

Bending, he slid his left arm under her shoulder, tilting her head so her hair fell away from her jaw, which was clenched, as if she were conscious and in pain, but her eyes were shut.

"*Shh*, lass," he whispered gently, not sure if she could hear him. " 'Twill be aright. I've got ye."

Gently, he straightened and sat on his heels, pulling her with him. She turned in his arms, her left arm still hidden under her body, and slowly opened her eyes.

He almost dropped her.

'Twas Skye MacIan; the woman who had been haunting his dreams for weeks.

"Where—where am I?" she murmured, lifting her right hand to her head, while her left swept around toward his side. Duncan felt something sharp poking him under his ribs, and just as soon as he could make his brain work, he'd figure out what that was.

But for now, *Skye MacIan* was in his arms, in the middle of the road, miles from her home.

"Lass?" he prompted her.

"I had the strangest—" She got a good look at him, and suddenly her eyes opened wide.

Trying to be helpful, he supplied, "Dream? Accident? Spiritual encounter with a saintly apparition? Gastrointestinal difficulties?"

Her eyes widened further. "*Shite.*"

Ah, so it *was* the gastrointestinal one. "Shite?"

She shook her head, and the sudden sharp prick in his side made him frown.

"Shite*shiteshitefook*."

Duncan's brows went up at her vocabulary. " 'Tis good to see ye too," he said drily.

"Put me down, ye great oaf."

Oaf?

He shook his head, realizing he was quite enjoying having her there in his arms. "Nay, no' until I ken ye're no' hurt."

"I'm no' hurt, but *ye* will be, if ye dinnae release me."

The way her gaze darted over his shoulder, then down to his side, had Duncan glancing down as well.

She was holding a dagger. A dagger which was currently pressed against his ribs, aimed for his heart.

"What are ye doing?" he asked mildly.

"I *was* robbing ye."

"What...alone?"

"Nay, laddie, no' alone," came the deep rumble from behind him.

Instinctively, he tried to shield the lass in his arms from whatever threat behind him might be, but when she jabbed him with that damn dagger again, he jerked back and loosened his hold on her.

When she kicked at him, Duncan fell back on his arse as she tried to scramble away from him. "By St. Simon's gilded piss, *what* in damnation are ye doing, lass?"

Even her frown was adorable. "Getting stuck in this bloody ridiculous gown, is what I'm doing," she muttered, her dagger not leaving her hand.

He was reaching for her, the primal need to help her overriding whatever threat she might claim to pose, when a shadow fell over them both.

"Here," the shadow grunted, manifesting a *huge* hand and reaching down to offer help to Skye.

She took the *shadow's* help, damn him, and stood with only a few curses.

And to Duncan's surprise, he found the idea of Skye MacIan—a proper lady—*cursing*, to be strangely arousing.

The sound of steel being drawn from leather dragged his attention away from Skye, who was trying to brush the dirt from her skirts. That silk molded to her in the most *interesting* ways, but the scowling older man with the sword made it difficult to focus on her.

"Ye're no' supposed to *cuddle* with her, ye *crumpety* clot-heid!"

Crumpety?

"I was no' cuddling with Skye," Duncan said, with an affronted air as he pushed himself to his feet. "I needed to make sure she wasnae hurt."

The older man jabbed forward with his sword, enough to make Duncan step back, but not close enough to hurt him. "Ye're no' supposed to ken her *name* either." He scowled at the mustached man by his side. "Pierre dinnae say aught of *kenning* ye."

At the accusation in his tone, the other man shrugged. *"Regardez combien son sac est lourd!"*

Duncan knew some French, thanks to his years studying with Master Claire. His right hand twitched toward his purse, while the other rested on the hilt of his sword.

"Ye really *are* bandits?"

The youngest member of their group shook his head. "We're *highwaymen.*"

"Oh, well, my apologies then." Duncan cut a glance at Skye, while also attempting to keep the other men in his sights. "Ye're a part of this?"

With a sigh, she jammed her dagger back in its sheath and planted her fists on her hips. "I'm their *leader*, ye bumbled-headed clackdish. And 'twas rotten luck Pierre chose *ye* as our next mark."

The MacIan Laird's sister was a highwayman?

*Nay. Look at her in that gown. She's verra much a highway*woman.

One he wouldn't mind cuddling with again.

Remember what happened last time ye tried?

Trying to convince himself his jaw didn't still ache from her blow, he inched closer to her, trying to keep from turning his back on the other men. "Skye..."

"*Custard!* Ye call her *Lady MacIan*!" the older man barked.

Duncan froze. "Aright," he agreed, with a deferential nod, not wanting to anger the madman who yelled about desserts. "*Lady MacIan*, might I have a word with ye?"

She hesitated a moment too long, before finally blowing out a breath. "Drop yer sword first. Fergus is verra protective of me."

Fergus was the sweets-lover?

With a blade pointed at him, Duncan realized he had little choice. Praying they weren't *really* after his purse, he unlaced his scabbard from his belt, then bent to place it on the ground.

His stepfather had made that sword for him, and if aught happened to it, there would be hell to pay.

When he straightened, glaring at Skye, she nodded firmly, then stepped away from her huge shadow. Duncan eyed the man—who hadn't said a word so far, but stood with his arms crossed and an affable expression on his face as he watched the clouds overhead—as he stepped around him.

Finally, he stood in front of Skye again. Lowering his voice—and his chin—he met her eyes. "*Lady MacIan*, what in the name of St. Simon's hairline is going *on* here? Ye're really the leader of this merry band of misfits?"

Something flashed in her eyes—he almost thought it was the look of shame, but he couldn't see Skye feeling shameful over anything—before she met his gaze angrily. "Aye, and what of it? We're highway-men, right enough."

Against his will, his eyes darted to where her breasts strained against the silk of her bodice. "*Woman.*"

Mayhap it had been the wrong thing to say, because with a snarl, Skye's hand shot out and closed around the leather pouch at his waist.

Before he could react, she'd wrenched the damn thing from his belt, yanking it toward her.

It was as if she'd pushed him in a frigid river.

Saints preserve me, she wasnae joking.

Skye MacIan, the laird's sister—Duncan's in-law—was indeed an outlaw.

He took a step closer, putting their chests almost inches apart. "Give that to me," he growled in a low voice.

She had the cheek to grin up at him, as if she understood the power had shifted. "Nay," she chirped, stepping to one side, which allowed her to lift the purse. "My, 'tis heavy, is it no'?"

As he swallowed down another angry protest, she loosened the strings and pulled the leather pouch open.

And whistled.

"What is it, milady?" the lad called from behind them. "Was Pierre right? Is that purse as heavy as it looks—"

"For the love of fig tarts, *shut yer mouth*, Rabbie!"

"Oui!" The Frenchman sounded excited. "*J'étais distrait par ma belle moustache.*"

"I dinnae ken," rumbled the giant for the first time. "Mayhap green. Or orange."

Duncan ignore them all. He *knew* what Skye was seeing, even before she poured the contents of the pouch into her other hand.

A fortnight before, Master Claire—the old goldsmith he'd apprenticed for years ago—had sent him to Eriboll to buy back some of her pieces. A merchant had died, leaving his wife with debts, and the widow was smart enough to offer Master Claire the chance to buy back the jewelry, instead of offering it to her debtors in place of coin.

Duncan had carried a small fortune to Eriboll, and had been successful in exchanging it for the finely wrought gold pieces.

There was the ring, set not with a jewel, but a delicate rose, fashioned from pounded leaves of gold. And a necklace, the heavy links making up most of the weight in Duncan's purse, regardless of the large pendant carved with the merchant's crest. And two brooches, one set with blood-red rubies, and the other a large pearl.

And a simple gold ring, made from braided strands, without any adornment.

It was the only piece Duncan himself had made.

Though one of his earlier works, he was still proud of it, even now, as it sat on top of a pile in Skye's hand.

She was staring down at it, and he could swear she wasn't breathing.

And why *shouldn't* she be frozen in pleased shock?

He frowned. 'Twas enough in her hands at that moment to keep an entire clan fed through the winter.

He had no idea what Master Claire intended to do with the pieces, but that was *her* business. All Duncan knew was that the gold wasn't his, and he *could not* allow it to be stolen by brigands.

Beautiful or nae.

So he took another step toward her. "Skye," he growled, "give those back."

Something changed in her expression, and she straightened her shoulders before finally looking back up at him.

He realized his mistake instantly.

If she really *was* the leader of this band, he shouldn't have challenged her like that.

Now she *had* to prove herself.

Shite.

"I dinnae realize the Oliphants hid such wealth," she called, louder than usual, as she held up the jewelry for her men to see.

Under the whistles and pleased hoots from the men behind him, Duncan cursed again.

When he took another step toward her, he was close enough to touch. Close enough to taste her scent; leather and pear, a scent uniquely her. Close enough to see her nostrils flare at his nearness.

"We *dinnae*," he growled again. "That doesnae belong to me, so I *cannae* allow ye to take it."

Instead of backing away, she lifted her chin and met his eyes with a smirk. "Too late, Duncan." She waggled the gold. "I've taken it already."

"Give it back."

Her giant loomed closer. "Want me to hit him, Skye?"

Now the three of them were locked in a contest of wills, and Duncan had a sinking feeling he was outnumbered.

But he wasn't going to lose Master Claire's work—at least not without a fight.

He held her glare, daring her to make a decision.

"Nay, Bean," she finally drawled, her blue eyes flashing in determination. "I think he'll be reasonable."

Duncan tried one more time. "For the sake of the family we share, return my master's art to me, and we can both be on our way."

There'd been a momentary softening of her fierce glare when he'd mentioned their connection, but her chin rose once more, her jaw tilted mulishly.

"My men and I work hard for our rewards, and 'tis been a long time since we took so fine a prize. With Hoarse Harold operating in the area, pickings have been slim. Ye'd have me just give up this opportunity?"

Oh well. He'd tried to play nice.

Time to bring out the big cannon.

"I do." When he grinned, he knew there was no humor in it. "Lest I report what I ken to yer brother."

There.

The way her gaze flickered, told him Laird Stewart MacIan knew naught of her little *hobby*, and she didn't want him to know.

"Ye wouldnae dare," she hissed.

"I would." He held out his hand. "Give me back my master's work."

"Want me to hit him, milady?" Bean rumbled again. "I could bop him on the head. Smoosh his skull. Make it look like an accident."

It was hard not to wince at that imagery, but Duncan managed it.

Skye, on the other hand, blew out an exasperated breath and glanced up at her bodyguard. "*How* exactly would it look like an accident?"

The man shrugged. "Maybe he accidentally ran into a rock."

"There's no big rocks around here, Bean."

"Maybe he accidentally ran into a big fist then."

It was the way Skye squeezed her eyes shut which made Duncan want to smile. She looked adorably frustrated, but obviously didn't want to roll her eyes at her friend.

"Skye," he prompted in a low voice, his open palm never wavering.

To her credit, she did glance down at it, and he thought she might be hesitating. The gold really wasn't his, and they *did* have a history together.

Not just because their twins were married to one another either.

Duncan had kissed her. He'd *tasted* that pear-and-leather scent against his lips and his tongue. He'd taken himself in hand as he'd imagined doing more—*so* much more to her—with his tongue and his hands and his cock.

Aye, they shared a history.

And mayhap that history was exactly why she wasn't going to back down now.

"Thank ye for yer offer, Bean," she said to the big man, while holding Duncan's gaze. "I'll take it into consideration. In the meantime, split these up, will ye?"

Duncan lunged forward, but he wasn't fast enough. She dropped Master Claire's jewels into Bean's hand, and Duncan's snatching motion came up empty.

As Bean turned and began tossing the pieces one-by-one to his compatriots, Duncan stepped up to Skye's side. With a growl, he reached an arm around her back and crushed her shoulder against his chest. Dropping his head, his lips were even with her ear when he whispered harshly, "Ye'll regret that."

The way she swallowed, told him she wasn't immune to his closeness, and *that* knowledge sent his blood to his cock.

Down, lad.

He had more important things to think about now, other than how good she felt in his arms, and how much he'd like to—

What in damnation did I just say?

Thankfully, his cock listened this time.

In order to meet his eyes, she had to tilt her head back and a little sideways, which left him staring down at the smooth golden skin, flowing down her neck and disappearing into her gown.

She didn't seem to mind.

"I dinnae see *how* I'll regret it, Oliphant," she murmured tauntingly. " 'Tis our practice to split up the prizes right away, because ye cannae fight *all* of us."

With that, he lifted his other palm to her cheek, so she was completely in his arms. As her eyes widened, he dragged that hand down to rest against her smooth throat.

"I dinnae have to," he murmured, knowing she was at his mercy. And knowing *she* knew that.

It was at that moment her men seemed to realize what was going on.

"Oi!" hollered the older man. "Ye step away from milady, ye crumpety oakcake!"

Before the last words had even left his mouth, Duncan had twisted, pulling Skye in front of him, her neck bent at an awkward angle, and her body between him and the rest of the brigands.

"Dinnae move," he snapped at them, his gaze sweeping over them all.

The older man was practically vibrating with anger, the tip of his sword swinging side to side. The giant stood with his mouth open, one of the golden brooches still cupped in his open palms, as if he were afraid to drop it. The Frenchman brandished two blades, but looked hesitant, which might be explained if he didn't really understand what was going on. And the lad was ignoring them all, studying the gold in his hand.

"Milady?" the giant finally rumbled.

"Easy, Bean," she choked out. " 'Twill— 'Twill be aright."

Of course it would, and if Skye really considered what she knew of him, she'd understand that. But Duncan was going to use this confusion to his advantage.

"Remove yer blade." His fingers pressed into her cheek. *"Slowly."* When she did, he eased his hold. "Now drop it."

Her men—all but the kid, who had eyes only for his prize—seemed to hold their breaths as she dropped her dagger away from her feet.

Were they waiting for a signal from her?

They weren't going to get it.

"Give me back my art," he said, addressing the oldest man.

With a clenched jaw, the man looked to Skye, who did her best to shake her head.

"G-get it to the clan, Fergus," she managed.

Shite.

She was planning on being stubborn.

But it was clear this Fergus cared for her and didn't want her to be hurt. And since he didn't know Duncan from a hole in the ground, so there was no reason for Fergus to think Duncan *wouldn't* hurt her.

And Duncan could use that assumption.

With a sudden sideways lunge, Duncan barreled into Bean, still holding Skye close to him. The big man stumbled backward, but not before Duncan grabbed the hilt of his sword.

As Bean fell on his arse, Duncan brandished the blade—

Or rather, the lack of a blade.

"What the—?"

The sword had been broken off six inches from the hilt, the remainder of the blade being the only thing keeping it in the scabbard.

Who in damnation carried around a broken blade?

As the giant lumbered to his feet, Duncan answered his own question.

A man even bigger than Rocque, who looks angry enough to eat ye.

Change of plans!

Tossing the broken blade aside, and holding Skye tight against him with his left hand, he whirled away from the stunned little group and lunged for the reins of his horse. As she cried, "*Nay!*" he swung aboard, pulling her unceremoniously across his lap, facedown.

"My art in exchange for yer mistress!" he called to her men, none of whom had a nearby horse.

Then he kicked his own animal into a gallop and, with her bouncing enticingly atop his thighs, headed for MacIan land.

He still wasn't sure of his plan—to have her alone, or to tell her brother of her escapades—but either way, he'd get his gold back.

And mayhap have the opportunity to kiss her again.

CHAPTER 3

Skye was so angry, she thought she might vomit.

Wait, no, that might be because she was *lying across a horse, for fook's sake!*

When Duncan kicked the poor thing into a gallop, she slammed down hard against his thighs, and didn't bother hiding the angry moan of protest which slipped from between her lips.

And then his hand dropped to her arse.

To steady her? Or for some other reason?

She vowed then and there, if he so much as squeezed, she'd make sure her vomit got *inside* those nice leather boots of his, by damnation!

Another jostle, and this time she cursed aloud.

How far had they ridden since he'd snatched her?

By the Virgin, *she* was the highwayman. *She* was supposed to be the one doing the kidnapping.

What other choice did ye leave him?

Squeezing her eyes shut to avoid the sight of the ground whizzing by so close, she told her subconscious to shut up.

She was a *thief*. This is what she did. She stole valuables from travelers to pay her clan's debts. Now that Fiona was married and wouldn't be able to use her charm to negotiate better prices for the goods they all needed, MacIan coin was even more dear. Skye *needed* this gold.

But from Duncan Oliphant?

He said the jewelry wasnae even his!

What did it matter who it belonged to?

'Twas hers now.

The horse turned with a lurch—why was Duncan leaving the main road?—and Skye muttered a curse as she began to slide across his lap...headfirst toward the ground.

She planted her elbows against the animal's flank just as Duncan grabbed the back of her belt. He didn't slow the horse, but at least he cared enough to keep Skye from sliding off.

What do ye expect?

He needs ye alive to trade for his gold.

Even as she struggled to push herself upright, a part of Skye knew Duncan wasn't going to hurt her. He'd held her neck—her *life*—in his hands just a moment before. He could've easily hurt her or worse, in order to retrieve his gold.

He hadn't.

Instead, there'd been something *besides* anger in his gaze when he'd looked at her.

Something which reminded her of their kiss.

Something which made heat pool between her legs, even as his stance held the promise of danger.

Oh, get yer mind out of the midden heap, lass, and get yer arse upright!

With another muttered curse—one even she herself could barely hear over the pounding of hoofs so close to her head—she straightened her arms, pushing against the horse and the stirrups, and even Duncan's leg, as she wriggled herself backward.

To her surprise, he helped, pulling her up, then holding her in place, when she was finally in a position to claw her way upright using the horse's mane. Duncan even helped her turn over.

But mayhap that was only because he wanted her *sitting* in his lap, instead of across it.

With a huff, she settled herself on her rear, both legs thrown over one of his, and tried to ignore how nice his arm felt across her back.

Was he helping support her, or was it just a natural place for his arm to rest?

Well.

Here she was.

In Duncan's *lap*.

Atop a galloping horse. Heading away from her men.

And Duncan had every right to be angry.

Blowing out another irritated breath, Skye reached up and dragged a handful of her hair over one shoulder, knowing, with it loose the way it was, it was likely blowing in his face.

"Let me go," she demanded firmly, making sure she spoke loudly enough to be heard over the pounding of horse's hooves.

When Duncan ignored her, she squirmed sideways, just a bit, in order to peek up at him.

He was staring straight ahead, but…was that a trace of a grin she saw on his lips?

"Let me go," she repeated.

"Try to behave, Skye."

Damnation, but *why* did his voice still make her insides go all squirmy?

She'd noticed it the day she'd met him in the stable of his ancestral keep. Of course, she'd thought him Finn then, the man her sister was hesitant about marrying. Skye shouldn't have kissed him back, but somehow the feel of his lips, the way his voice reached down deep into her stomach and *squeezed*, made her forget her loyalties for a time.

When he'd kissed her again, she'd damned well remembered then.

Frowning, she blew out a frustrated breath.

If she hadn't been watching him, she would've missed the way his gaze dropped to her lips for only a moment, before snapping forward once more. And then his lips twitched. "Ye're a shite highwayman, Skye."

"Excuse me! I am a brilliant highwayman. *Woman*," she hastily corrected, not liking the way her heart had jumped at the sight of his smile. "I just dinnae expect to see *ye*."

Determined to get in the last word, she twisted, planting her shoulder blade against his chest and lifting her left knee over the front of the saddle. This way, she was still facing ahead, but without having to straddle the horse's neck in this damnable gown.

The gown!

It was a garish crimson, something her sister-in-law had commissioned in order to show Skye was *the sister of a great laird*. Please. The MacIans were barely surviving since Allison had married into the family.

What *did* that woman find so much to spend MacIan coin on?

Focus, lass.

The gown was brightly colored and especially useful in attracting the attention of potential prizes. And it would be equally helpful in attracting the attention of her men.

Because Skye *knew* Fergus would be coming after her. He might be a bit behind, because Duncan's animal was still galloping, and Fergus and the others would have had to go round up their horses, but he *would* follow.

And a part of Skye knew it'd be easier to just give the man his bloody gold back and let him be on his way. But another, more stubborn, part of her wanted to send the gold back to MacIan land with Fergus, so she could stay with Duncan a bit longer—

What? Nay!

Nay, he'd *kidnapped* her!

After ye waylaid him and relieved him of his coin.

He'd called it his *art*. Glancing down at her hand, at the simple braided-gold ring she'd slid on her finger, before tossing the rest to Bean, Skye knew that was the correct term for it. This *was* art.

Focus, for fook's sake!

Oh, aye, the gown.

And mayhap there was a way to hide the ring she'd stolen, as well…

Keeping her hands low, certain her shoulders would block her movements, Skye very carefully tore a strip of crimson silk from the hem of her gown, then nonchalantly dropped it from the horse.

She didn't dare turn to see where it had landed, but prayed it would help Fergus find her.

But would it be enough?

Nay, he'd only know she *passed* this way, but not where they were going. She'd need to continue dropping cloth for him to follow their trail.

The second piece she ripped she made sure was long enough to reach around her neck, then, slowly, keeping her movements as small as possible, she slid the ring from her finger and onto the red silk ribbon.

Then she pretended to sneeze, and in lifting her hands to her face, hurried to slip the ribbon around her neck, under her hair, and tie it in the front.

There. Smooth as a baby's bottom.

The third and fourth pieces were easy to tear and drop over the side of the horse, leaving a sort of trail. But then she reached a seam, and when she yanked on it, harder than intended, two things happened.

One, she elbowed Duncan in the side, and he grunted beside her ear.

Two, her bloody dress ripped all the way up the side, to at least her knee.

Freezing, she held her breath, waiting for him to catch on to her scheme and say something.

When he didn't, she cautiously returned to her work, picking at the threads with her fingernails, until a strip ripped away from her gown along where the seam had been. It might've made a noise, but she was certain he couldn't hear it over the sound of the horse.

Otherwise he would've said something, right?

By the twelfth time she'd dropped a piece of crimson silk, the sun was low in the horizon, and the front of her gown's skirt was almost in tatters. Luckily, the way she was sitting had made it easy for her to go about her efforts, but she was going to have to switch positions soon, so she could reach another section of her gown.

Duncan chose that moment to slow the horse again, having alternated between cantering and trotting over the last hour.

For what seemed like the first time since he'd snatched her up, Skye felt him relax. The breath he blew out ruffled her hair, and she remembered she'd tucked as much as she could down her bodice to keep it from blowing around.

With a low groan, he twisted first one way, then the other, stretching his muscles. Then he settled easily into the saddle once more, but she continued to hold herself stiffly away from him, wondering what his plan was.

His right hand—which had been resting on his hip as he rode—now came around to take the reins from his other hand. And for a moment, she was enclosed in his embrace, surrounded by his warmth.

And when he dropped his right arm, she vowed she wasn't disappointed.

Oh, aye.

But his right hand came to rest on her hip. Just...rested there. Not possessive, not threatening, but just resting there, as if his hand belonged on her. As if it was perfectly normal for him to be touching her so intimately.

And part of her agreed.

"So…" When he spoke, his breath tickled the back of her ear, the same way that delicious, gravely tone of his tickled *other* parts of her. "Are ye going to continue?"

She jerked, partly in confusion, partly because she'd allowed herself to relax against him. "What?"

The hand on her hip didn't move, but she could hear the humor in his voice when he answered.

"Ye're running out of silk. I thought mayhap ye'd like to turn a bit so ye could reach a different part of yer skirt. Or…" When his voice lowered, so did his chin. She could *feel* his breath against the back of her neck now, as if he were staring down the front of her gown. "Or mayhap yer bodice?"

"Ye want me to start ripping apart my bodice?" she asked in a choked voice.

She felt him shrug. " 'Twas just a suggestion. I wouldnae mind if ye did, but 'tisnae necessary."

Blessed Virgin! What was he saying? "Why is it no' necessary?"

"Because I've left a trail a blind man could follow."

Oh, joy, here came her anger, bubbling back up again, after being repressed for so long by being able to actually *do* something.

"Ye *want* my men to follow us," she accused in a hot tone. "That's why ye havenae stopped me ripping up my gown."

This time, he didn't so much shrug, as shift in the saddle, and she clamped down on any pleasure she *might* have gained by feeling his hard thighs move under hers.

And—curse him!—his hand began to move against her. Just slightly, his thumb making small, comforting movements against her hip.

She tried not to enjoy it.

"I'd be lying if I said I didnae want ye, Skye Maclan," he finally admitted with that low, rumbling voice of his.

And she was almost positive she managed to clamp down on the whimper of yearning his little confession provoked.

"But?" she managed in a strangled whisper.

"*But*...I also want my master's art back. And I can trade ye for those pieces."

And damn her, but an indignant snort burst from her lips. "Ye want that gold more than ye want me?"

As soon as the indignant question had left her lips, she clamped them down hard against each other and prayed he wouldn't answer.

But then, after a full minute went by and he *didn't* answer, she got angry again.

"Am I wrong?" she turned in his lap, trying to glare at him, but was unable to make it all the way around. Instead, she twisted her neck enough to meet his eyes. "Am I?"

When he dropped his gaze to hers, Skye knew she was in trouble.

Those beautiful dark eyes of his would be her undoing, even more so with the unrecognizable emotion in them now. His blond hair was as long as his brother's, but Duncan kept it tied back at the base of his neck. It made him look refined, which was a delightful, delicious juxtaposition to how callused his hands were from his work at the forge.

Whoa there, lass. Ye're no' planning on eating *the man, are ye?*

Her eyes widened, remembering some stories her sister had told her about the marriage bed, and she whirled back around, pressing her shoulders to his chest and trying to hide the heat in her cheeks.

"Ye punched me."

His whisper had been so faint, she wasn't sure she'd really heard it.

"I thought ye were Finn," she snapped, the excuse obvious and half-hearted.

He made a noise, which might've been an agreement...or mayhap not.

Weeks ago, Skye had joined her identical twin sister, Fiona, as she traveled to Oliphant Castle to marry one of the laird's sons, Finn. In the courtyard, Finn had reached for *Skye*, thinking her Fiona, which had led to some awkwardness.

Not an hour later, Skye had been in the stable, caring for her horse, when Finn—or at least a man who had looked exactly like Finn—had begun flirting with her.

She couldn't deny her attraction, and had known her sister wasn't devoted to the idea of marriage, so she'd felt it safe to flirt back. And when he'd kissed her, she'd kissed him back...until she'd come to her senses.

The guilt had eaten at her, and she'd tried to tell Fiona, several times, that her husband-to-be was complete pond-scum, but her sister had pushed her away each time.

Then came the night Skye had left the room to Fiona for privacy and had slept in the stables. The very morning after her sister had given herself to Finn, Skye woke to find herself in his arms.

So she'd punched him.

It wasn't until later that morning, when she'd seen Finn standing beside *his* identical twin, that she'd realized what must have happened.

And standing there in that great hall, her arms around Fiona as she watched both men lift their identical kilts to show off almost-identical dangly bits—Finn apparently had a freckle, but Skye hadn't peered too closely, due to being distracted by *Duncan*—she'd been surprised by the relief she'd felt.

Aye, she'd punched Duncan Oliphant for taking advantage of her...but now that she knew who he was, she'd gladly allow it again. If only he hadn't run off to Eriboll so quickly.

She'd been a little hurt by that, to tell the truth.

But she wasn't about to tell *him* that. "Why'd ye run off to Eriboll, Dunc?"

The nickname came easily, half-mocking, half-affectionate. He was silent for a long moment.

"My master sent me," he finally said. "One of her patrons was interested in selling back the work she'd done for him, and she's too old to make the journey."

"Yer smithing master is a *woman?*"

"Aye." The pride in his voice was obvious. "She's the best in the Highlands, as far as I'm concerned. My stepfather was the first to put a hammer in my hand, but Master Claire taught me patience and craft."

She'd met his stepfather—the village smith was even bigger than Laird Oliphant—a fortnight before, when she'd visited his smithy to ask about caltrops. They were vicious tools she refused to use, but Hoarse Harold often employed them. If she could only figure out where he was getting them from...

"She lives in Lairg. That's where I was headed the first day I met ye. Finn wanted me to stay and meet his betrothed, but with Master Claire getting up there in years, I felt I had to rush to Lairg to see why she'd summoned me." His thumb was making those little circles on her hip again, and she wondered if he was doing it on purpose. "I'd just returned, the morning I found ye sleeping in the stables."

Finn had explained all this, *after* Duncan had escaped Oliphant land once again.

"So the gold ye carry…"

"Master Claire's, aye," his low voice rumbled behind her, lulling her into a false sense of relaxation. "I carried enough coin north to buy the pieces from her patron's widow, who needed the monies more than the gold, and was kind enough to offer the exchange. On the trip back, I kenned I needed to stay alert for bandits, but I dinnae expect them to be so pretty."

Wonderful.

So now she had to feel guilty of not only stealing his gold, but of stealing an *old woman's* artwork?

Damnation.

With a sigh, he tugged her closer, and she was too surprised to resist. In the time it took his breath to rustle her hair, his left hand was spread across her stomach, her back was flush against his chest, and her arse was nestled atop his—his *hardness*.

With his chin, he nudged her head to one side, and she found herself leaning against him. It was wonderful. It was terrible.

"What kind of woman turns highwayman?" he murmured in a speculative voice, as if the answer didn't really matter. "I kenned ye fierce, lass, but why turn to thieving?"

Because I'm desperate.

But there was a part of her, warm and safe and content in his arms, which scoffed at her own thoughts. So she pressed her lips together and said nothing.

Instead, Skye simply allowed herself to enjoy his embrace and pretend he cared about her, if even only a little.

CHAPTER 4

ST. SIMON'S LEFT BOLLOCK, but she felt *right* in his arms.

Too bad *she* would rather be anywhere but in his arms right now. 'Twas obvious from the way she'd done her best to leave a trail her men could follow. And as much as Duncan claimed he wanted her men to follow that trail as well, a bigger—*harder*—part of him wanted as much time alone with her as possible.

It was that hard part, currently pressing against her arse, which probably clued her in.

"So," she began, as she squirmed in his lap, "if ye get yer gold back, what will Master Claire do with it?"

He tightened his hold on her, warning her without words to quit moving. Not because he wanted to control her, but the way her thighs were pressed against him, had him painfully hard already, and her movements weren't helping matters.

"I dinnae ken," he murmured, trying not to breathe in her leather and pear scent. "Mayhap sell to another patron."

"Claire made all those pieces?"

For some reason, the knowledge Skye remembered his master's name, and was clearly impressed with the woman, made him smile.

"Most of them," he said nonchalantly. Only one piece had been made by him, and he didn't know which of her men held it. "All but the simplest ring. I made that one when I was learning the craft."

She hesitated, then asked a little too quickly, "How did ye meet Claire?"

If she wanted to hear him talk, he'd oblige her. The sun was setting, and he had every intention of stopping for the night soon, but he'd look for some food for them first.

"My mother lived in the village below Oliphant Castle. As soon as we were born, Da began to visit us. My brothers, Alistair and Kiergan, were already living up at the castle—they're two months older than us, and their mother died giving birth to them. By the time we were weaned, the four of us were a 'roaming pack o' ruffians,' to hear Da tell it."

Smiling, he remembered the trouble they'd gotten into as lads and all the mischief they'd caused. But he wasn't answering her question.

"Our mother married the smith, a good man—"

"Edward," she interrupted, sounding pleased she knew at least some part of his tale. "I met him."

"Och, aye, Mam said ye'd stopped by to visit." She'd said it with a twinkle in her eye, come to think of it. "Asking Edward about caltrops, she said?"

Skye shifted her weight again, causing him to spread his fingers across her belly. When she sucked in a breath, he wondered if he'd startled her, or if she *liked* his touch.

"Hoarse Harold has been kenned to use the devilish little devices, and we cannae track where he's having them made. My men have searched from Wick to Eriboll, and nae smith will admit to making them for him."

Duncan hummed thoughtfully. "Neither Edward nor I would make them."

Caltrops were simple tools and required no skill or finesse to create; they were simply two sharp nails, bent around one another, to form four points across two planes. No matter how they landed on the ground, one of the sharp points was always pointed upward.

Run a horse across a scattering of them, and you could lame the poor beast. And even if you didn't permanently harm the animal, you'd still end up stopped there in the middle of the road.

Hoarse Harold, and other highwaymen, had made particularly effective use of them.

"So ye've never used them?"

She straightened so suddenly, it made him realize two things: One, she was genuinely offended by the question; and two, she'd been bloody relaxed in his arms until that moment.

"I would *never* harm a horse that way!" she hissed.

"Easy, lass," he murmured. "Ye have my apologies." His tone turned teasing. "What else was I to ask, having such a dangerous, *brilliant* highwayman in my arms?"

Slowly, she exhaled; her shoulders slumping against his once more. "Ye were telling me about yer stepfather."

Changing the subject, aye?

He chuckled, then gave her what she asked for. "Edward was the one who'd seen I needed direction, or I'd become as shiftless as Kiergan. By my second month apprenticing with him, he realized I had an eye for detail he lacked, and put me to work on the smaller projects, which required more patience. And by the time I was thirteen, he'd found Master Claire—who'd just retired—and sent me to study with her. In a year, I was producing the jewelry she could nae longer create."

Skye didn't speak for a long time.

When she finally did, Duncan had just spotted the smoke from a crofter's hut and veered toward it. She'd relaxed against him again, and he wondered if she noticed.

"Yer family cares for ye, even yer stepfather."

"Aye," he blurted, startled at the wonder in her tone, "of course he does. We're family."

When she didn't respond, he flexed his fingers against her belly, the gentle movement not quite a massage. "Yer brother loves ye too, I ken it."

The memory of standing there in the great hall, Duncan's kilt up around his ears, still made his neck flush. But he knew Stewart

MacIan had only forced the issue, because he cared for Fiona's future, as he surely cared for Skye the same way.

"Fiona and I are the youngest of eight. Stewart became laird when our father died, and our two sisters had already married by then. Two of our brothers joined the church, and one died before I was old enough to remember him. None of us are close."

It was the sadness in her voice which made his protective instincts flare. He had a twin brother and eight other siblings in total, counting Nessa and Mam's bairns by Edward. He was lucky enough to have two families and couldn't imagine not being close to *any* of them.

"I'm sorry, lass. At least ye have Fiona."

"Nay, *Finn* has Fiona now."

St. Simon's spleen, she sounded pitiful.

"Still, yer brother, the laird, cares for ye. Even if ye're no' close, he's honor-bound to protect ye." Seemed like as good a time as any to ask the question which had been gnawing at him. "So why in damnation are ye *thieving* like a common bandit?"

It was Duncan's incredibly bad luck that the horse trotted up to the crofter's yard at that moment.

"I'm *anything* but common, Duncan Oliphant," Skye declared in a haughty voice, as she sat forward, pulling away from him. "Now, if ye're going to fetch us something to eat, ye best do it quick, afore darkness falls."

Damnation, but she was right.

As he slid his hand away from her, he gave her hip a little pinch. "Dinnae do aught stupid, lass," he whispered, as he slid from the saddle, taking care to reposition her *and* keep a firm hold on the reins as he stepped up to the croft.

When the crofter stepped out, he eyed the Oliphant plaid Duncan wore, his shoulders relaxing. "What can I do for ye?"

"Might we buy some food off ye?" Duncan asked, doing his best impression of his brother's charming smile. "The lady and I are hungry."

The man's gaze flicked to Skye, who sat haughtily atop the horse in her now tattered silk gown. Still, he didn't comment on the claim she was a lady, and instead dipped his chin. " 'Twill cost ye."

And of course, Duncan had no purse. Hoping the man would be amenable to trade, he simply nodded in return.

"The missus made bread today," the man said with a grunt. "And she can wrap up some of the fish me lad caught."

"We would be grateful, sir," Duncan said with another nod.

"Three coins for the lot of it."

Duncan hid his wince. He was about to offer his finely tooled sword belt—which was useless now that his fine sword was lying in the dirt of the road where he was attacked—when Skye interrupted him.

"Seven coins!"

What?

Duncan half-turned, sending her a glare.

By St. Simon's uvula, *what* was she doing?

But the crofter, clearly enjoying the idea of bartering, was quick to snap in return, "Four coins!"

Squinting in surprise, Duncan gaped at the man.

Did he not realize Skye had bid *up*?

Apparently not, because Skye hummed, as if pondering. "I can go as low as six."

"Six? *Bah!*" the man spat. "Five, and 'tis my final offer."

Wait, what?

The man had been willing to accept three coins not a minute ago, but thanks to Skye...

Duncan turned back to the horse to see her perched up there like a queen. A queen who looked only a mere moment from laughter, and *quite* proud of herself.

It was that pride which had him smiling in return. "Who taught ye to haggle, lass? Ye're bad at it. Ye're a verra bad haggler."

Her chin rose, and she met his gaze with twinkling blue eyes. " 'Tis my duty to make things hard for my captor, is it no'?" she said in a low voice, as the crofter ducked into his home to gather the food.

Knowing they were alone for a moment, and knowing he could

make her blush, Duncan winked.

"Och, lass. Ye're making things *verra* hard for me right now, if ye ken my meaning."

She didn't blush.

Well, she *did*, but to Duncan's surprise, her gaze darted to his kilt, and when she looked back at him, there was something very much like anticipation in her eyes.

HE WAS STILL THINKING about that look an hour later, when he decided to stop for the night. It was dark enough, and he didn't want to push the poor horse any further. And besides, there hadn't been any sign of a pursuit.

Which was a little odd, all things considered.

"Are we going to stop for the night?" Skye asked in a treacly voice.

He wasn't fooled. Not by this, or the half-dozen other tests she'd masked as insults since leaving the crofter's hut. He wondered if she realized yet they were heading for MacIan land...and if not, what she'd do when she did.

For that matter, Duncan wondered what *he'd* do. He wasn't *really* planning on turning her over to her brother for punishment...was he?

If only he knew *why* she'd turned highwayman!

But she was still waiting for an answer from him.

"Aye," he sighed. "We'll stop and wait for yer men to catch up."

In fact, there was a likely-looking copse of trees just up ahead, which was set back from the road and would offer some sort of protection, but still near enough he should be able to hear them coming.

"And we're waiting for them, because ye're sick of being with me?"

With a smile, he swung down from the horse. "Nay, lass. Being with ye is like being drunk. I cannae be sick of it. Until I am."

In the waning light, he thought he saw her frown as he reached up for her.

"Was that an insult?"

By St. Simon's armpit, she felt good in his arms!

He pulled her from the horse and placed her on the ground between him and the animal, keeping hold of her as she got her footing.

And then a bit more.

She *was* frowning, aye, as she stared up at him. So he smiled in return.

"I suppose 'twas. I dinnae *like* being drunk."

"Yer brothers do, for certes."

Well *that* surprised a burst of laughter out of him, and he finally dropped his hands from her waist and stepped to the side to untie the bundle of food from the saddle, which had cost him his sword belt after all.

"No' all of them drink," he began in a nonchalant tone, hoping she understood he was just trying to set them both at ease. "Malcolm is the scholar of our bunch. He'd much rather be scribbling notes or inventing a new kind of lantern than drinking."

Behind him, she'd moved away, stepping into the clearing and kicking at the coals from the last traveler's campfire. "Aright. That's one—two, counting ye—out of six."

"And Alistair doesnae indulge, because he's too busy keeping the clan running. He's the one in charge of our finances and futures more often than no'."

Sensing it was a good time to try to get more answers from her, Duncan turned, food in hand, to see her kicking some stones into a circle around the coals.

"Do the MacIans have a seneschal? Or does Stewart handle the clan's funds?"

She glanced up at him. "If ye're asking if he'd notice the coin and gold I bring in, the answer's nay. We list it in the books as coming from one of the outlying properties, and he's never bothered to check."

Duncan opened his mouth to ask, once again, *why* she felt it necessary to thieve, when she began heading for the shadows of the trees. "Where are ye going?" he blurted instead.

"I have to piss," she called over her shoulder.

"Wait!"

When she turned with a huff, her fists on her hips, he felt his lips pull upward. "Ye expect me to allow ye to just gallivant off St. Simon-kens-where? I need to keep an eye on ye, if I'm to have any chance of retrieving my master's art."

She blew out a breath. "I'll count out loud. But I do have needs to see to, ye ken."

"Count?" Pursing his lips, he pretended to think it over, as he propped his foot up on a tree stump. "Nay, that willnae do. Ye'll have to sing."

"Sing…?" she repeated flatly.

He smiled. "Aye, sing! Good luck."

He was laying out the bread and fish—and discovered the crofter's wife had included some early-harvest apples as well—when her voice rang through the trees.

No one would ever accuse Skye MacIan of having a dulcet-toned singing voice, but she'd likely chosen the most vulgar song she could think of, simply in an attempt to irritate him.

It was the one he'd been singing himself, just that very morning.

"Her stockings 'round her ankles and her shift oot o'the waaaaaayyyyyy. I grabbed her 'bout the arsecheeks, and that's when I heard her saaaaaaaaaaaaaayyyyyyyyyyyyyyy!"

Chuckling now, Duncan joined her in the chorus, certain she was the most interesting lass he'd ever met.

"Ooooh, buck-a-diddle-diddle, buck-a-dilly-ay—"

His laughter drowned out her curses of displeasure, and soon, she rushed back into the clearing. It was hard to see her expression in the dim light, but from the way she had her hands planted on her hips, he could tell she was angry.

"Ye *ken* that one?" she barked.

"Ye're unlikely to find a song I *dinnae* ken, lass," he said, still chuckling. "Da taught us that one years ago." Beckoning toward the food, he sank down to his haunches beside the stump.

"All of ye?" she asked, as she crossed the clearing.

He waited until she snatched up a piece of the bread, then took his own. While she remained standing, he made himself comfortable, with his back against the remnants of the old tree.

"Nay, just Kiergan and I, as I recall. Kiergan, of course, was more interested in the *mechanics* of the lyrics, while I was fascinated with anything musical."

She watched him in silence as she ate. Finally, she swallowed. "Ye're an artist, are ye no'? Interested in songs and creating things?"

He had to think about her words for a moment, before finally shrugging. "Aye, I suppose so. Rocque has tried to teach me a warrior's ways, St. Simon kens it, but..." He took another bite of the bread. "But I'm nae warrior," he revealed, around the mouthful.

Instead of mocking him, Skye hummed thoughtfully. "Rocque is the brother who's so big?"

"Malcolm's twin, aye. The two of them look as unalike as Finn and I are identical. But they're closer than any of the rest of us."

"And Rocque is the Oliphant commander, aye?" Mayhap she was more at ease with this topic, because she sat down on the stump, near enough to him, so all he would have to do is twist his head to be able to kiss her knee.

If he *wanted* to kiss her knee.

There's other places I'd rather kiss.

Wait, what was it she asked about?

Oh, aye, Rocque.

"He's been training the men since we were lads, feels like, but Da made him commander a few years back. *He's* the warrior in the family, right enough. And he's almost as big as *yer* man...*Bean*, was it?" Something had been bothering him since they'd made their escape. "Speaking of Bean, *why*, in all that's holy, is his sword broken?"

Though he wasn't facing her, he could *hear* the smile in her voice when she replied.

"Did ye see the size of his fists? The dear man doesnae *need* a sword. He broke it years ago, but when he tried to go around without it, he said he missed the feel of the scabbard at his side."

"I suppose I can understand that." Duncan finished his bread and wiped his hands together to dust the crumbs from them. "Are ye ready for the fish?"

"I'm no' hungry," she said quietly.

He couldn't tell if she was lying, but he wasn't about to push her. The lass had made the choice to become a *highwayman*, by St. Simon's kneecap, and he knew she was no weakling. If she didn't want to eat, then she didn't want to eat...so he reached for the dried fish for himself.

While he chewed, she stood and brushed the crumbs from her gown. The sight of all that ruined silk actually made him smile, because it was a symbol of her ingenuity, certainty, and downright bollocks.

It wasn't until she began to shuffle about the clearing—hearing the *swish* as she used her feet to check for obstacles, because the moon hadn't risen with enough light to see by yet—that he steered the conversation back to where he wanted it.

"Rocque is my father's commander. Is Bean the MacIan's commander?"

He couldn't *see* her look of disgust, but he could feel it. And even though Duncan knew she couldn't see him either, he still hid his smile by biting into the bland fish.

"Broad shoulders doesnae make a man a leader, Dunc." She sounded exasperated. "Bean is a sweetheart, aye, but he's as dumb as a sheep stuck in a bog."

"So sheep stuck in bogs are dumb then?"

She clucked her tongue as she turned back to her task. " 'Tis clear ye're nae crofter."

And *she* was?

He loved the way she stood up to him, the way she matched him—blow for blow and wit for wit.

"I was merely wondering if yer brother—or his commander, or seneschal, or whatever—kens what ye and Bean, and the rest of them, are up to."

Her foot ran into a branch, and he could see her silhouette as she bent over to pick it up. "And if he doesnae, ye'll be the one to tell him? Ye'll run to him, because *ye* are somehow the one who gets to determine how I live my life? *Bah.*" She broke the branch in half and tossed both pieces toward the old campfire.

"Mayhap," he said, noncommittally, as he finished off the piece of fish and reached for the other. "But I'm no' yer keeper."

Although I wouldnae mind.

Where had *that* thought come from?

He *wanted* to be with her?

"Damn right ye're no'." She bent to pick up another stick. "Ye have a big enough family, Dunc. Just because my sister is married to yer brother doesnae make *us* family." The sound of the wood breaking punctuated her irritation. "Ye can just mind yer own bloody damn business, with yer half-drunk brothers and yer daft aunt yelling, '*Doooooom!*' all the time, and that stupid drummer of yers."

Duncan's brows had risen the second time she'd used his old nickname, and when she began listing the particularities of life at Oliphant Castle, his lips twitched.

"Ye've heard him?"

"Who?" she snapped, crouching to collect a handful of twigs.

"The drummer."

"Aye— *Nay*" Skye muttered, as she stalked toward the ashes to drop her newest collection atop the other sticks she'd already gathered. " 'Tis daft to think a ghost warns of doom."

"Aunt Agatha claims only those who are doomed to fall in love will hear the drummer, Skye. Did yer sister tell ye that?"

From the way she wrapped her arms around her middle, he suspected Fiona had.

In a small voice, Skye asked, "Have *ye* heard him?"

"The drummer?" He'd been hearing him more and more frequently since the summer had started, and up until that moment, he hadn't stopped to consider why. But all he said in reply was, "Aye."

And from the way her shoulders slumped, he knew for certain she'd heard the ghostly drummer of Oliphant Castle as well.

"What are ye doing with all this wood?" As if he couldn't guess.

She crouched down and began laying the twigs. "I'm making a fire, since ye cannae be arsed to do it."

Smiling, he stretched his legs out in front of him, and crossed one booted ankle over the other. "We dinnae need a fire."

She stood so fast, and inhaled a gasp so sudden, Duncan wondered if she went light-headed.

"Nae fire?" she repeated.

Slowly, Duncan's lips stretched, and he stacked his hands behind his head. "*Nae fire.* I ken ye only want to set one to alert yer men. Well, *I* want a decent night's sleep, and I'll no' get it if I have to worry about that Bean of yers breaking my head, or yer Frenchmen stabbing me in my sleep."

She planted her hands on her hips again. " 'Tis *Fergus* ye have to worry about, but ye're wrong; I wasnae going to alert them. I was— I was *cold*."

Och, now he *knew* she was lying.

"Come here, lass," he beckoned, with a low voice, as he dropped his hands to pat the not-very-comfortable dirt beside him.

"Why?"

She sounds mulish.

He couldn't keep the laughter from escaping. "Because I'll keep ye warm."

With a muttered curse, and a sigh of surrender, she stomped over to him. He took this as a good sign, because surely she wouldn't sit so close to him if she were afraid of him, no matter what…would she?

But when she sank down beside him, her silk-swathed arm brushed against his, and he sucked in a breath. She *was* cold, and he instantly felt like an arse for not believing her.

So without a second thought, he reached one arm around her and snugged her up close to his side.

And she allowed it without argument.

"Ye smell like fish," was all she muttered.

"I'm saving the apples for the morning to break our fast," he tossed back at her, realizing she was only satisfied when they were arguing.

She'd take his comfort and warmth, but she refused to let him know she appreciated it. He knew that much about her at least.

Neither spoke for a while, and when her cheek dropped to his shoulder, he wondered if she were sleeping. But her breathing hadn't evened out yet, so he decided to help her along.

"Both Finn and Fiona heard the drummer, ye ken. They might've already been in love, but the drummer sealed their fates."

When she hummed, he *felt* it.

"They were already pledged to one another." She yawned. "The betrothal was just a formality."

After the last kiss he'd shared with Skye—when she'd punched him—she'd run to her sister and told Fiona that *Finn* had been the one to kiss her. Which had understandably broken Fiona's heart, considering she and Finn had spent the following night together.

Once *that* particular comedy of errors had been resolved, Stewart hadn't been convinced *Finn* had been the one to take Fiona's virginity, and had demanded both brothers lift their kilts, right there in the great hall—in front of all, including the Lord himself—to determine which brother was which.

It had been humiliating for certes, though he could now admit it had been a bit funny. And when Skye's shocked eyes had landed on his dangly bits, the scene had become more than a little arousing.

In fact, just the memory was doing wonders for him right at that moment.

Shifting, he tried to adjust his cock into a more comfortable position, without doing something so crass as to alert her by using his free hand.

What had they been talking about?

Oh, aye, Finn's betrothal.

"When Da told us his plan—his *ultimatum*, really—Finn was the first one to jump at the opportunity. He'd been wanting to marry yer sister since the day he'd met her."

Skye snuggled a little closer, and Duncan swore his heart skipped a beat.

"I heard about yer Da's plan when I was at Oliphant Castle. He expects ye all to marry? And the first to have a son will be laird?"

He snorted, half in agreement, half in dismissal. "As if we all *wanted* to be laird!"

"Ye dinnae?"

He jerked in surprise. "*Nay.*" When he turned to stare at her, his chin slammed into her forehead, and she jerked as well. "Would *ye?*"

She sat up, rubbing her forehead. "Want to be laird? Nay."

"What about a laird's wife?"

He couldn't see her expression, but the slightly bitter tone of her laughter answered his question, making her next words unnecessary.

"I have enough responsibility, thankyeverramuch."

"Sorry," he muttered, pulling her back toward him once more. "What *do* ye want? In life, I mean. Is being a highwayman yer ultimate goal?"

To his surprise, instead of resting her head on his shoulder again, she placed one hand on his chest, shifted, twisted, and somehow ended up curled up…with her head on his thigh.

Her head—her *mouth*—was just inches away from his hardening cock, and inside his head, he rattled off a string of curses.

Apparently, *she* wasn't affected by the proximity, because she answered him with no problem.

"I dinnae ken."

What in damnation had they been speaking of?

All of Duncan's blood had apparently drained away from his brain.

"I guess I never really gave a thought to my future," she continued.

Oh, aye, that's *what we were talking about.*

"Now that Fiona is married, I suppose Stewart will do his best to get rid of me."

Sitting there in the darkness, mayhap 'twas easier for her to speak of these sorts of things.

Duncan's hand fell to her shoulder, then ran down her arm, doing his best to warm her, and willing his cock to behave.

"He'll sign a betrothal contract for ye?"

Her little half-shrug seemed almost defeated. "Or a convent."

Well, hell.

"I suppose the life of a highwayman has its appeal, when faced with those two options," he admitted quietly. "Does he no' notice yer absences?"

"We're never gone for more than a night, and nay, I doubt he—or anyone else back at home—notices me much at all," she finished in a whisper.

"Then to hell with them," Duncan blurted, with more passion than he'd intended. "They'd have to be *blind* no' to notice ye, Skye."

Duncan suspected *he'd* have to be dead and buried before he could ever stop noticing her.

The silence—broken only by the call of an owl off in the distance —stretched long enough, he wondered if she'd fallen asleep. He kept his hand moving slowly over her arm, offering what little comfort he could. Hoping not to jar her too much, he wriggled his way down the stump behind him and propped his head against it.

When she spoke, he tensed, startled.

"How about ye, Dunc? Have ye chosen a woman to marry?"

Back to speaking of Da's decision, eh?

Duncan sighed. "Nay. I dinnae like the idea of him choosing my future for me, but I ken why he did it. If I *do* follow his directive and marry, I'm no' sure who I'd choose."

Suddenly, he was struck with the sure and certain knowledge those words were a lie.

He *did* know who he'd choose…may God have mercy on him.

"What kind of woman are ye looking for?" she murmured.

"A straightforward one, and one who's no' afraid of a challenge," he began hesitantly, wondering if she'd recognize who he described. "No' flighty, no' concerned with fashion or afraid of hard work. I live in a *smithy*, by St. Simon's beard!"

"Ye'll still live there, once ye're married?

He'd never thought of his future, beyond being a smithy that is, but as he tried to spin the idea, to paint the picture in his mind for Skye, an image began to solidify.

"I suppose I'll need a cottage near the smithy." As the possibilities came to him, his voice got surer. "My mother and her husband live near his smithy. My wife would have to be happy in a cottage like that, a *life* like that, because I'll no' be the laird if I can help it."

She snorted softly, and he thought it was a snore, until she spoke. " 'Tis no' something ye can help, no' if ye plan on sleeping with her."

"Sleeping with her?"

"*Sex*, Dunc," she corrected sleepily. "If ye fook her, ye'll get her pregnant eventually."

There were ways to ensure it didn't happen, at least long enough to saddle one of his brothers with the responsibility of lairdship. But the very *last* thing he needed to do was talk about sex with this intriguing, beguiling, confusing woman.

"The point is, she'd have to be happy and content no' to be the wife of a laird. She'd have to be content with *me*."

"Ye?" she yawned.

"*Me*." Duncan closed his eyes and rested his head back on the stump. He was surprised to find this vision of his possible future made him smile. "A simple man. No' a warrior, but a man who works with his hands. A *creator*, no' a destroyer."

With a little sound, which might've been a purr, might've been a hum, Skye shifted and snuggled even closer to him, the crown of her head pressing against his bollocks. But rather than sending a spike of lust through him, this time, the position was almost comforting.

Duncan realized, more than anything, he wanted to be lying there on the cold, hard ground with her. He wanted to wrap himself around her to keep her warm, to keep her comfortable.

Skye was a stubborn, headstrong woman, and Duncan suddenly realized *he* wanted to be the one to take care of her, even though he knew she would insist she could take care of herself.

His hand dragged down her arm again. "I ken no' all women want marriage and babies and housework, Skye," he whispered. "But my wife would still have to be content with me. No' gallivanting all over creation."

Not robbing travelers. Not putting herself in danger.

In other words, he realized even more, as his eyes closed in sleep, *not Skye*.

CHAPTER 5

Skye was warm...and cozy. It reminded her of one of those cold winter mornings, when she'd wake to find Fiona plastered against her back.

In her half-awake state, she realized it was *exactly* like that, because only her back was warm. Whatever was beneath her stretched-out body was hard, and something heavy was atop her, hugging her stomach.

Disgruntled, she let out a little moan and began the torturous, ungainly process of rolling over. Her gown stuck beneath her, and Skye knew it wasn't going to happen gracefully, but soon she'd be able to press her face against whatever heat source was—

Oh!

Her eyes flew open as soon as her cheek hit his chest and she inhaled his unique musk and—

How *did* he still manage to smell of wood ash and ale?

She was sleeping with Duncan.

He was keeping her warm.

More importantly, he was keeping her *safe*, having wrapped himself around her on the hard ground, one arm thrown over her hips now, but what had once been the heaviness she'd felt on her stomach. He'd moved it as she moved, and now his hand dangled against the small of her back.

Not holding her captive, but just resting there. As if it belonged.

Strangely, Skye hadn't tensed at the realization she was cuddled up against him. Strangely, this felt...*right*.

Last night she'd laid her head in his lap, close enough she could brush her cheek against his manly parts—the ones she'd already seen and been fascinated by...and had hardly stopped thinking about since.

She remembered he'd been speaking when she began to doze off, so she closed her eyes, inhaling the scent of his chest, and tried to recall their conversation.

He'd been telling her about his ideal wife, hadn't he?

Duncan had said he'd be content with a wife who was content with *him*. He'd understood not all women were the same—Skye couldn't sew to save her life!—but he expected his wife to stay home and take care of him.

Isn't that what he'd said?

It was hard to remember, because she'd been so close to sleep when he'd been speaking. But also, it was hard to *think* with him so close to her.

Carefully, she stretched her legs out, following his, until her slippered feet brushed against his calves, then she scooted her hips closer to his.

For warmth.

Although she was quite warm as it was. With the sun rising, the air was warming wonderfully.

Although...*mayhap* there was another reason she was warm; a reason which had to do with the way his hand flexed across her back, suddenly pulling her closer.

Or mayhap it had something to do with the way his breath hitched when hers did.

Or mayhap it was the way the hard length of him pressed against her belly.

God help her, she knew what *that* was. She regretted her hands were trapped between their chests, because Skye *itched* to reach lower and pull up his kilt so she could hold and examine him. She'd seen his —his *cock*, but now she felt it.

And she wanted it.

Desperately.

Overcome by the sudden and overwhelming need, a whimper escaped her lips as she instinctively pressed her pelvis forward.

He jerked as if he'd been burned.

"Where the hell are yer men?" he muttered.

Well, for certes, she hadn't expected *that* response!

"What?"

"Yer men," he repeated, as he rolled away from her. "I left a trail even a three-legged donkey could follow."

His words barely registered, as a burst of disappointment swept over her at his abandonment.

Duncan pushed himself to his feet and began brushing off his plaid as he retreated into the woods to take care of personal business. As she sat up and pulled her knees to her chest—surprised at how chilled she suddenly was—Skye couldn't help noticing he hadn't so much as looked her way.

Was he so anxious to get rid of her?

It was obvious, from his body's reaction, he wasn't *completely* disgusted by her presence.

Or had that simply been an involuntary thing?

Could it be he hadn't forgiven her for the punch, back when she'd mistakenly, though understandably, thought he was his brother?

Skye wished *she* could so easily dismiss her body's reaction to *him*.

As she watched, he emerged from the trees and crossed to where he'd pulled the horse's saddle from its back the previous night, and began to dig around in one of the bags.

It was clear by his slow movements and lackadaisical attitude, Duncan intended for her men to catch up with them.

Why?

"Want an apple?" he called out, still not looking at her.

Clearing her throat, she pushed herself upright, the tatters of her red gown getting in her way. "In a moment," she replied, in as much of a controlled voice as she could manage, refusing to let him see how much his indifference hurt her.

This time, he didn't make her sing when she went into the woods to see to her needs. Whereas last night she'd been thinking about ways to escape, now she only wanted to hurry and get back.

Back to him.

Even though it was clear he wanted nothing to do with her.

She forced herself to take her time, to brush the dirt from her gown, to breathe deeply.

I can do this. I can walk back over to him and no' *show him how disgustingly attracted I am to him. Here I am, taking another deep breath. Here I am, pretending naught is wrong. I can do this.*

She couldn't do this.

As soon as he looked up and met her eyes, her knees went weak and she stumbled.

And despite the fact she *knew* he wanted naught to do with her, he lunged forward, stopping the motion only when he saw her right herself.

They met, not in the middle of the clearing, but beside a large tree trunk, halfway between where the horse stood and where they'd woken.

Duncan was holding an apple at chest-height, a few bites taken from it.

Well, he did *offer it to me.*

With a mischievous grin, Skye reached up and placed her hand around his. He didn't flinch, and she took that as a good sign.

Ye've seen naught yet.

Holding his gaze, knowing she was playing with fire, she tugged his hand—and the apple—toward her mouth.

His dark eyes went wide as she bit into the apple, the juice running down his fingers. When his lips parted, and his gaze dropped to her mouth, she knew he wasn't unaffected.

But was he as aroused as *she* was?

Emboldened, she took another bite, hardly tasting the crisp fruit. Then she pushed his hand toward his own mouth, leading the apple to his lips, and urging him with her eyes to take a bite.

And when his lips pulled back, baring his teeth to clamp down around the faded red skin of the apple, she felt the jolt all the way down to the junction of her thighs.

Holding her gaze, he chewed, and—*Blessed Virgin*—but she could *see* the challenge in his gaze.

And she wanted to meet it.

Lifting her other hand, she wrapped it around his thick wrist, both hands now tugging the fruit to her.

But when she licked her lips, savoring the taste of the juice, he growled something which might've been a curse, and jerked forward, tossing the apple aside and twisting his arm in her hold, until he was cupping her cheek.

He was going to kiss her! She *knew* it!

But then...he didn't.

He halted, his lips just inches away, as his eyes darted back and forth between hers.

"What are ye waiting for?" she whispered.

His gaze dropped to her lips, so she licked them again for good measure.

He groaned. "Ye ken what I think?"

Knowing she was taunting him, she took a breath, parting her lips slightly and thrusting her breasts toward him. "Nay."

"I think ye're impulsive and wild."

"Ye think I dinnae ken what I'm doing?"

"By St. Simon's heart, lass, I think ye ken *exactly* what ye're doing." His gaze snapped back up to hers. "And so do I."

Before she could question him, he'd dropped his hands to hers, his callused fingers closing around her wrists and tugging her sideways. A startled gasp escaped her, but not as much as the breath which whooshed out of her, as he pushed her against the tree and locked her hands together above her head.

Instinctively, she tugged, trying to get loose, but he held both of her wrists easily in one of his own, and stepped closer.

And she realized she wasn't scared. Not even a little bit. She was this man's captive, but the reason her blood was suddenly pounding in her ears was more due to anticipation than fear.

So she lifted her chin, and didn't bother to hide the way she was panting, when she met his eyes.

"I'm no' afraid of ye."

"Ye should be," he growled.

This was Duncan Oliphant. They might not be on the best of terms, but her heart knew his. He *would not* hurt her.

And besides, she found she was aroused as hell by this side of him.

Skye tugged at her hands again. "Let me go." She tried to make the command sound seductive and failed, but at least she didn't sound scared.

"Nay, lass. I cannae afford to have ye hit me again." His gaze caressed her face, mostly her lips. "Of course," he murmured, "I cannae afford to kiss ye either."

But then…he did.

When his lips lowered to hers—*finally!*—Skye surged to meet him. This kiss was like the ones they'd shared in the stables at Oliphant Castle; hot and desperate, knowing their time together would be over at any moment.

But God help her, she loved it.

She loved the taste of him, the apple still crisp on his tongue. She loved the way his tongue teased her as he pulled her deeper into his embrace. She loved the way he only touched her at the wrists and the lips, until his other hand dropped to her hip, as if to hold her in place. She loved the way her little whimper of need drove him against her.

She loved everything about this kiss.

With her hands pinned above her head, she couldn't pull him closer, but she thrust herself against him, the want—the *need*—pulling another moan from the back of her throat.

He was a smith; a master of fire and molten metal.

And he'd turned her into both of those things; made her so very desperate for his touch.

The liquid heat pooling between her thighs reminded her of the way she'd touched herself, thinking of him. Then, she'd only had the *memory* of his kisses, but *now*...!

Blessed Virgin, she wanted him. Wanted *all* of him.

And his thick member pressing against her hip told her *he* wanted her too.

She pushed against him again, gyrating her pelvis, in a poor approximation of what she needed from him.

But he pulled away, breaking their kiss with a gasp.

She followed, leaning forward as if she could hold onto the kiss, the confusion breaking through the arousal. As the haze cleared from her vision, her chest heaved, and she met his eyes.

But instead of the disgust she was afraid she'd see there, all she saw in those dark depths was...

Pain?

Why?

Why didn't he want her?

Her wrists were still held in an iron-strong grip above her head, the bark from the tree scraping at the backs of her hands in the most delicious sensation.

Testing him, she pushed against his chest to see if he'd release her. His grip only tightened, and her heart jumped.

He wanted her.

His hard cock was pressed against her, and *he wanted her*. He didn't want to let her go.

She swallowed, trying to find the words to get what she needed. "I want—" She swallowed again and forced the words out. "I want ye to kiss me again," she whispered.

His gaze held her as captive as his hands did. "I want that too."

Then why didn't he?

"Do ye want me to beg?" As desperate as she was at that moment, she would.

Now he was staring at her lips. "God," he whispered harshly, "ye're too proud to beg."

She was just drawing breath to refute that claim, when, with a groan, he slammed his lips down atop hers once again.

This time, she *tasted* his need as he pressed against her. This kiss was frantic; the pulsing in her temples matched the throbbing between her thighs.

Was he as desperate as she was?

From the way he groaned, Skye hoped so.

Duncan shifted, and his hard length nestled against her, right where she needed the pressure.

The sensation shot straight from her skin to her brain, and she broke away with a gasp.

They were both panting heavily, even as she thrust her pelvis against him, again and again, mimicking what she really wanted.

"*Duncan!*" she moaned. "I need... I *need...!*"

His grip loosened on her wrists, even as he tightened his hold on her hip, pulling her closer against his cock.

"Aye, lass?" he managed with a choked voice, dropping his forehead to hers. "What do ye need?"

Oh God.

"I need..."

With a moan, she pulled her hands free and dropped them to her sides, frantically pulling her gown up, desperate to press her fingers into her aching core.

But somehow, his kilt became tangled with her skirts, and instead of lifting her silk, she lifted his plaid.

And then she was standing, pressed against the tree, holding his kilt above his thighs, and she stopped thinking.

Reaching for his thickness was instinctual, and as her fingers wrapped around it, he sucked in a startled gasp and reared back.

But she didn't give him time to object; didn't want him to back away, not when she was finally able to explore what she'd seen a fortnight ago in his ancestral great hall.

It took both her hands to hold him, to cup his bollocks, as he stared at her in disbelief.

"Skye, I—"

"Shh." She leaned forward and planted a kiss on his jaw, which was as far as she could reach.

But when he surrendered with a groan and leaned forward once more, resting his weight on the hand which was braced against the tree above her head, she placed a kiss on his neck. Then his throat, then his chest.

Blessed Virgin, his skin tasted as good as his lips did!

And his cock…?

She slid one hand along its length, marveling at how smooth it was for something so hard. She'd *seen* it, and felt it pressing against her. But *holding* it was entirely different.

It was everything she'd hoped it would be.

"Skye…" He groaned again, closing his eyes, as he dropped his head forward.

He was entirely at her mercy, and that knowledge was more arousing than anything else.

"I want ye, Dunc," she whispered, barely audible. She was breathing too hard to know if he heard her, though she wasn't all too sure she wanted him to. "I have since— God help me, I want ye!"

From the way he swallowed—the stubbled column of his throat moving heavily so close to her lips—she knew he'd heard her for sure this time. She continued to stroke him, marveling at the moisture which had gathered at the tip of his cock, her fingertip spreading it around.

"This isnae— *Skye*…"

The way he moaned her name reached down between her thighs and pulled *hard*. She dropped one hand away from his cock to reach for her own core through the layers of silk and linen. She cupped herself, pushing the heel of her hand against her bead of pleasure, and pressing her fingertips into her wet warmth.

He must've seen what she was doing, because with a sudden curse, he pushed away from the tree. But instead of leaving her, instead of pulling away, he dropped one hand atop hers, and his other hand...

Well, he wrapped his other hand around hers, where it curled around his cock.

And then he was staring at her, his face curiously blank as he showed her how to stroke, faster and faster, his cock caught between them. The fingers of his other hand curled around hers, as thick and strong as the rest of him, pressing her gown into the center of her pleasure.

The pressure was building under the heel of her hand, under his fingers. Instinctually, she flexed against the sensation, her pelvis moving in the same pattern as her hand on his cock. Her chest tightened as the pleasure built inside her, more and more desperate for release.

The pace of their breathing increased, matching one another, until his breath caught completely.

And then wet warmth spilled over her hand, and she twitched forward.

The knowledge she'd just brought him to release, while holding his gaze, sent her over the edge. As her lips parted on a little whimper, she came undone against his hand as well.

Both of them jerked toward one another, breathing heavily, as they broke their staring contest.

She planted her forehead against his shoulder, and he loosened her hand—her *pleasure*—to prop his hand above her head and lean against the tree once more.

"*St. Simon's tits,* Skye!" came his strangled whisper. "Ye just jerked me off like—"

Like a whore?

Her face hidden against him, she didn't bother holding in her wince. Still, she wasn't one to back down, and as he'd noted, she *was* impulsive.

"Like *what*?" she mumbled the challenge.

"Like I was a green lad," he finished with a sigh, lifting his head. "Do ye ken how long 'tis been since I soiled my kilt this way?"

Well, if he wanted to joke about it…

She lifted her head too, her heartbeat still not back to normal yet. "Dinnae fash. I think as long as ye wash the damn thing yerself, yer mam will never ken."

The laugh which whooshed out of him was part surprised, part sarcastic, as he straightened away from the tree.

"I am sorry I put ye in a position to think—"

She never found out what he was apologizing for, because hoof-beats interrupted them.

Duncan spun around, his kilt falling back into place as he crouched slightly and flexed his arms, standing between her and whatever danger approached.

But as her men rode into sight, she stepped out from behind him, meeting Fergus's gaze and willing him to understand she was fine.

"Fooking poor timing," Duncan muttered, his hands curled into fists.

She hummed, doing her best to surreptitiously straighten her gown and pluck leaves from her hair. "I dinnae ken. Ten minutes ago, I would've called it 'fooking poor timing.' "

His grunt sounded as though it might've been an agreement as he straightened from his crouch.

"Milady!" Fergus shouted, swinging down from his horse before the thing had fully stopped. "Are ye hurt? Did this honied fruit-cake of a custard hurt ye?" His eyes frantically darted across her ripped gown, to her swollen lips. "I'll kill the tarting bastard!"

Yesterday, she'd been ready to steal Duncan's gold and leave him. Today, *now*…

Skye straightened her shoulders and took a deep breath. After the time she'd spent with him yesterday, the way he'd protected her and cared for her, even though she was his prisoner, the way she'd come apart under his fingers and felt his release in her hand…?

Well, saying things had changed would be the mildest way to put it.

"Peace, Fergus," she called, one palm out. Her gaze took in the rest of her men, who'd now appeared. "I am well."

She stepped up beside Duncan, shoulder to shoulder, and prepared to lie.

"Duncan Oliphant is my brother-in-law." *More or less.* "And my time with him has reminded me of my responsibilities, even if he is no' a MacIan."

Atop his huge horse, Bean shifted uneasily. "Milady?" he rumbled; his big hand clasped around the hilt of his broken sword.

She gentled her tone. "Give Duncan back his gold, Bean." Her gaze swept her men. "All of ye."

Fergus glared at Duncan. "What did ye do?"

And Duncan, bless him, merely shrugged. "My master's art for the return of yer mistress. 'Twas the deal all along."

"*Fig tart,*" Fergus muttered, then whirled back to the other men and jammed his sword into the scabbard.

Skye had just enough time to exchange a glance with Duncan— filled with uncertainty and about a thousand things she wished they'd had time to say to one another—before Fergus began to bark orders.

"Ye heard the plumcake! Hand it back over! Come on, Rabbie!"

With various levels of grumbling, the men pulled out Duncan's gold and tossed or handed it to Fergus. Beside her, she could *feel* Dunc holding his breath.

The older man at last turned back, his cupped hands brimming with the gold jewelry, and was glaring daggers at Duncan, who slowly exhaled in relief.

But was he relieved to have his master's art back, or relieved to be getting rid of her?

"*Oatcake!*" Fergus cursed, tossing the gold to the ground in front of Duncan.

But instead of bending to pick it up, he—the man who'd just brought her the most intense climax she could recall—turned to look at her. His dark eyes were inscrutable, but she thought she saw sorrow in their depth.

Sorrow he was getting what he wanted?

Or, like her, was he sorry their time together had been interrupted?

Still, she couldn't allow him to think she lacked control...control over her men or over her own emotions.

He called ye impulsive.

But she didn't *have* to be.

So instead of grabbing his ears and pulling him down into another soul-searing kiss, she lifted her chin and reminded herself she *was* in control. "What took ye clot-heids so long? I was stuck with this pile of dog's vomit for *too* long. Ye were supposed to come after us!"

It was Rabbie who whined, " 'Twasnae our fault, milady."

Crossing his arms in front of his chest, Pierre controlled his horse with only his knees. *"Je pense que j'ai une éruption cutanée sur mes fesses."*

Bean nodded. "Aye, Hoarse Harold is a right pickle."

"Hoarse Harold?" Skye's gaze slammed back to Fergus. "Ye ran into Hoarse Harold?"

The older man looked abashed as he hooked his thumbs into his belt and hung his head. "Aye, milady. No' long after we fetched the horses and came after ye, he and his *fig tart* men stopped us."

When he paused his story, Skye lurched toward him, her arms out. *"And?"*

Fergus shrugged. "And what?"

"And *what bloody well* happened?" Her eyes darted over her men, looking for wounds, and when she found none, she began to breathe easier. "He didnae take Dunc's gold or yer purses?"

"Nous avons battu Harold comme une laitière faisant du beurre!"

She didn't even bother glancing at Pierre, but kept her attention on Fergus, who shrugged again.

"He only had two tarting henchmen with him, and both of them will need priest robes."

Skye gaped. "Ye killed them?" she whispered.

In all her time as a highwayman, she and her men had killed no one. They hadn't even seriously *harmed* a victim.

But Hoarse Harold's men didn't really count, did they?

It was Rabbie who answered proudly. "We didnae kill them, but *I* cut one of them badly. Bean knocked the other one senseless."

"But..." She shook her head. "The priest?"

"*Ils portaient des robes!*"

Fergus nodded. "They were all dressed in custardy monk's robes. Or priests. I can't berries-and-cream tell the difference, can I? Anyhow, they bled all over them and will need new ones."

Blessed Virgin.

Skye blew out a breath and glanced at Duncan. He stood now, his arms folded across his chest, eying her men, clearly not caring about their brush with one of the Highland's most notorious highwaymen.

She tried not to notice the way his position accentuated his shoulders, or the way it made the muscles in his strong arms bulge.

She tried not to think of the way those callused hands would feel upon her skin.

She failed, and judging from the way his brow twitched at her, he knew it.

Whirling back to her men, she stalked to where Bean held the reins to her horse. "Did ye bring Duncan's sword?"

"Ye mean the pile of dog's vomit's sword, milady?"

The giant's tone was innocent, but she could tell he was teasing her. "Aye, that one," she snapped.

"Nay, but I brought mine."

Bean patted the hilt in his scabbard, and she forced an approving nod, knowing that's what he hoped for, before swinging herself up onto the saddle.

They'd returned Duncan's gold. They'd escaped Hoarse Harold's clutches.

And Skye?

Well, Skye suspected her life had changed significantly within the last day. Since she'd opened her eyes to see a concerned Duncan Oliphant bending over her, she knew she was in trouble.

Since then, he'd held her, protected her, teased her, kissed her, made her feel…well, he'd made her *feel*.

Meeting his eyes across the clearing, Skye swallowed.

Somehow, she knew that warmth, that spark, that *arousal* she felt with Duncan was unique. She was certain she'd never find anything close to the same with another man, and since he was the one man she couldn't have…she would have to remember this morning for the rest of her life.

Because that was all she would ever have.

Clenching her jaw, she wondered if he could see her sorrow, but hoped he couldn't.

"Come on," she whispered, shaking her head, as she pulled her horse's reins to the right. "Let's go home."

CHAPTER 6

CLANG!

Duncan's hammer smashed into the soft metal, again and again, shaping the sword as well as he could.

His stepfather, Edward, had always taught him 'twas foolish to attempt to force steel to do his bidding when he was angry.

The metal demands respect and a clear mind.

Well, to hell with that!

Duncan slammed the hammer down again, reveling in the burn of his muscles and the sweat pouring down his back. He'd tied a scrap of cloth around his forehead to keep his eyes clear, but he needn't have bothered.

With the way he was feeling now, he didn't need *sight* to shape the sword. He barely needed touch.

Really, all he needed was a hammer, some sparks, and a reason to hit something.

"St. John's warts, Brother, what's gotten into ye?"

Panting, Duncan straightened, throwing a scowl over his shoulder at Rocque, who merely raised a brow in return.

Mayhap if he ignored his brother, Rocque would take the hint and go away.

It didn't work.

"Ye've been moping since ye returned from Eriboll two days ago. And now I'm getting complaints of the noise ye're making, smithing this late at night."

Ignoring Rocque, Duncan lifted the steel in the prongs, turning it this way and that, looking for defects. He was used to dealing with smaller amounts of metal, smaller tools, and more delicate movements. But 'twas hard to deny the satisfaction which came from slamming something molten and stubborn.

"Dunc," his brother sighed, "ignoring me willnae help. Da wants to ken why ye're moping—"

"I'm no' moping," Duncan growled, as he hefted the hammer once more. "And since when do ye do Da's bidding?"

As the hammer *clanged* home once more, Rocque ambled into Duncan's line of sight. The bigger Oliphant brother shrugged and crossed his arms, propping a hip against Edward's anvil and watching Duncan's work.

After a long while—punctuated by the hammer's blows—Rocque changed the subject. "Ye're making yerself a new sword?"

Frowning, Duncan lifted it again for an examination, and blew out a breath. " 'Tis shoddy workmanship." He shook his head and tossed the hammer down. "Edward always said no' to work angry, or this is what ye'll get."

"So ye're *angry*, no' moping?"

Angrier still to be caught in the verbal trap—and by *Rocque*, no less—Duncan scowled. "Why are ye here, exactly?"

His brother shrugged again, then nodded to the blade. "I wanted to ken what ye were making. And what happened in Eriboll. I've never kenned ye to be so…" It looked as if he wanted to say one thing, but hesitated. Instead, he finished with, "*Angry.*"

Duncan muttered a curse and plunged the sword back into the fire. Mayhap he'd be able to breathe easier—and *focus*—if he talked to someone about the churning of emotions in his gut.

" 'Tis a woman," he finally admitted with a sigh, eying his brother to see what Rocque's reaction would be.

To his surprise, his larger brother simply grunted and shifted into a more comfortable position. "Ye met her in Eriboll?"

"Nay, I..." Duncan paused as he pulled the rag from around his head and ran his hand through his hair. "I kenned her earlier, but I ran into her on the journey home."

He wasn't sure why he was keeping Skye's identity a secret, but he hadn't even mentioned to Fiona he'd seen her twin. And since it was damned hard to look at his brother's wife without thinking of the way Skye had kissed him, or taken him in her hands, or had smiled at him...

St. Simon's sacred thighbone, he was getting hard just thinking of her!

The last two days, since returning home, had been...difficult, to say the least. He'd more or less hidden himself in the smithy, much to Edward—and wee Ned's—consternation. But any time he had to see his twin brother's delirious happiness with a woman who looked exactly like Skye MacIan, he wanted to punch something.

Which was unlike him.

But it *was* like Rocque, so Duncan wondered if his brother may have some suggestions for how to deal with all these—these—*feelings.*

"Do ye ever get so angry, ye just want to...to... I dinnae ken."

Rocque's laughter burst out of him, sharp and quick. "Och, aye. All the time. 'Tis why Da made me the Oliphant commander, ye ken."

"Because ye're angry?"

"Nay." The big man grinned. "Because I frequently want to hit someone."

"And do ye ever..." Shaking his head, Duncan pulled the blade from the coals to check the intensity of its heat. "Do ye ever think mayhap God put lasses here on earth just to anger us?"

Rocque didn't respond, but when Dunc looked up at him, his brother was grinning broadly. At Duncan's raised brow, Rocque chuckled.

"Have ye no' met my Merewyn? She angers me at least once a day."

Most of the village knew of Rocque's battles with his hot-tempered mistress, the local healer and midwife. But the pair seemed content.

"And despite her angering ye, ye still love her?"

Rocque shrugged and pushed himself to his feet. "I dinnae ken about love, but she's a good lass. And arguments are fine, when ye can be promised to make up the way we do."

When he winked, Duncan scowled.

Which caused his brother to chuckle once more. "Ye look like a man who's been angered by a lass, and no' had the chance to *make up*. What did she do to ye, this mystery woman?"

" 'Tis no'—" Duncan shook his head, then wiped the sweat out of his eyes with the rag, wondering if he was going to get his sword finished tonight. "I'm no' angered at *her*, so much as the circumstance."

His brother hummed in understanding. "Ye want her, but ye cannae have her?"

How'd Rocque guess that?

Duncan wiped his hands down his kilt—a new one, because *aye*, he'd had to clean the old one, thanks to Skye's touch, and 'twas still drying—and reached for his hammer.

"Ye might look like a boulder, Rocque, but ye've got a brain in that hard head, huh?"

"Och, nay. My uncle used to say the only thing my head was good for was hitting things."

That shot another spike of anger through Duncan, and he hid it by slamming the hammer against the anvil as he pulled the blade from the coals.

Everyone at Oliphant Castle knew Rocque and his twin, Malcolm, had been raised away from their clan. Their maternal grandfather had banished their mother when he'd discovered her pregnancy, and the twins had been born in the home of a distant relative—not truly an uncle, but that's what they still called him—who'd treated all three of them like dog shite. When their mother died, the lads eventually made their way back home, where the rest of the Oliphant bastards had welcomed them the way true brothers did.

For another long while, the only sound was the hammer shaping the metal. Eventually the familiar motions began to sooth Duncan, and he was able to forget about his brother's past, Skye's deed, and the future.

Until Rocque finally spoke.

"Why no' marry the lass?"

The hammer slipped from his hand and narrowly missed his foot.

"*What?*" Duncan growled as he bent to pick up the damnable thing.

Rocque, the complete donkey's bollocks, merely shrugged. "Marry her. Da says we all have to marry, so why no' the woman who has ye so wound up ye cannae tell yer arse from a hole in the ground?"

"*First* of all"—Duncan pointed at his brother with the hammer —"*that* makes nae sense. Second of all, do ye no' think I've considered that? *Bah!*" He turned back to his anvil, and took a deep breath. "We wouldnae suit. And there are other…complications."

"Are ye certain ye wouldnae suit? I might've thought the same with my Merewyn, but we get along fine."

"Well, why do ye no' marry *her*?" Dunc snapped.

Rocque's grin grew. "Mayhap I *will*. But we're speaking of ye. What are the complications?"

She's a highwayman.

She willnae tell me why.

She makes me forget my own name when she kisses me.

Even now I want her.

"Fook," he whispered.

"Aye!" Rocque chuckled, then crossed the smithy to slap Duncan on the shoulder. "Complications are complicated, but ye'll never ken for certain ye'd suit just fine, unless ye quit yer moping and go *ask* her."

Duncan shrugged off his brother's hand. " 'Tis no' that simple."

But Rocque was chuckling as he headed for the door. "Ye dinnae ken that. The way ye look right now, I'd say there's something verra simple the two of ye have in common, and it has everything to do with yer cock. Figure out how to make it work, Dunc."

"Dinnae call me that," Duncan muttered reflexively, remembering the way the nickname sounded coming from Skye's lips.

Remembering *everything* about Skye's lips.

Rocque stuck his head back in the smithy. "Oh! And, Dunc?" He jerked his chin to the half-forged blade on the anvil. "Dinnae give any of my men that piece of crap. We'll stick with Edward's swords, thank ye verra much."

When Duncan lifted the hammer threateningly, as if he would throw it across the space, Rocque ducked out, his laughter following him.

Figure out how to make it work.

Duncan stared down at the red-hot blade—not his best work, he could admit.

Make it work.

Could he?

He swallowed. Da had told him he had to marry, and while the idea had been horrifying when he'd first heard the demand, since meeting Skye...

Well, being *commanded* to marry was still frustrating, but he could understand how two people might want to agree to spend the rest of their lives together.

But would *she* marry *him*?

He snorted to himself as he plunged the blade back into the coals.

Marry him?

She'd likely chase him from her family's keep with her own blade.

But...

But she—or rather, her men—still had something which belonged to him. He'd been able to return all of Master Claire's work to the elderly goldsmith, and was thankful the only missing piece was the simple braided ring he'd made.

It had taken him almost until Lairg—and it was bloody uncomfortable to ride a horse with the inside of his kilt being as sticky as it was—to count the gold pieces he'd been returned. Only one was missing, and he wondered who had it.

That ring would be the excuse he needed to go to the MacIan keep. To see *her*.

To get some answers.

To *see* her.

To ask her to marry him.

To see—

Nay. *Nay*, he didn't just want to *see* her. He wanted to taste her, to feel her, to *love* her.

St. Simon's left bollock, *love*?

Shaking his head, Duncan blew out a breath and pulled the blade from the fire. He had a lot of thinking to do.

"Ow! Ye're gripping my chin too tightly!" Allison scolded, pulling out of Skye's hold.

Skye gritted her teeth, knowing full well that she was in full view of her sister-in-law, and thus, couldn't roll her eyes the way she wanted to. "I need ye to hold still."

Allison narrowed her eyes. "I can hold still just fine without ye leaving bruises on my fair skin. What would yer brother say if I told him *ye* were the one to hurt me so?"

"What would he say if yer eyebrows grew together atop yer face like some kind of bushy orange worm?" Skye snapped in returned.

Her sister-in-law reared back with a gasp, and rage flashed in her brown eyes. For a moment, Skye tightened her grip on the tweezer in her hand, not sure if Allison was going to slap her, or burst into tears.

Either was possible, as the MacIan twins had learned over the last year, ever since Laird Stewart MacIan had married the woman. Allison was the eldest daughter of a smaller clan, but despite the MacIans' hardships, she seemed to think she were now just as high and mighty as the Earl of Sutherland.

Instead of lashing out this time, Allison's eyes filled with tears.

Shite.

When Allison cried, Stewart gave her anything she wanted.

Which is why we've barely enough to support the clan as 'tis!

"I cannae believe ye'd say something so cruel to yer verra own sister," Allison sniffed.

This time, Skye couldn't stop her eyes from rolling, but she turned away under the pretense of reaching for a wet cloth so Allison wouldn't see it.

"Ye're married to my brother." 'Twas as close as she'd come to telling the manipulative bitch she was no sister of hers. "And I told ye I'd help ye, because ye cannae pluck yer own brows yerself. But ye *have* to hold still."

"Well, *ye're* the one ripping hairs out of my face!"

Snorting, Skye tossed her the rag, ignoring Allison's shriek of protest as the water splashed her.

"Aye, and it'll hurt. 'Tis the price ye pay for beauty."

Allison pressed the cool material to her forehead and sighed mightily as Skye crossed back to where she was sitting, wielding the tweezers like a blade.

Her sister-in-law had remarkable carrot-orange hair, and rather unfortunate eyebrows to go with it. And since falling pregnant, her hair and nails have grown at prodigious rates. Her curls were thick and luxurious...but so were her eyebrows.

Allison must've been thinking the same thing. "For certes, breeding comes with its own collection of trials nae one tells ye about." She sighed dramatically from under the cloth. "But 'tis worth it—"

Skye had heard this last part enough to be able to mouth the words along with her sister-in-law. And as Allison's eyes were covered by the cloth, Skye did so.

"—to bear the next laird of such a great and powerful clan."

With a sigh, Skye settled herself in front of her brother's very pregnant wife—the heart of all the clan's current troubles—and lifted the tweezers once more.

"Are ye ready, Allison?"

"Oh, verra well." Allison lowered the cloth and lifted her chin, her eyes closed. "The price we must pay for beauty."

This time Skye was careful not to grip Allison's chin too hard as she tilted the other woman's face back to catch the morning light from the window.

How in damnation do I get stuck doing this each time?

Allison likely viewed it as a bonding experience. Or else she just didn't want her maid to see her this vulnerable.

At least she's willing to come to my room, instead of dragging me to hers. Last time I went there, I had to hear all about her physical relationship with my brother. Ew!

The tweezers were sharp, and she was able to grab three of Allison's carrot-orange hairs—the ones growing right above the bridge of her nose—and yank them out all at once. Her sister-in-law flinched, but didn't cry out, and Skye knew 'twas mean-spirited to take even the tiniest bit of pleasure in Allison's discomfort.

But she did anyhow.

"Do ye think we'll be done soon? I have an appointment."

An appointment?

"Where would ye be going?" Skye murmured, her attention on the left brow.

"Oh, um." This time when Allison flinched, Skye got the impression it was because she'd said more than she'd intended. "I told a—a *friend* I'd pick up something for him from the blacksmith."

Skye straightened, frowning down at her sister-by-marriage.

Why would Lady MacIan need something from the *blacksmith*?

"What are ye picking up?"

Allison peeked open one eye. "Caltrops," she answered in a breezy voice, as if trying to dismiss it as silly. "Silly things, are they no'?"

Frowning, Skye bent down once more. "Aye," she murmured.

She and her men had spent ages trying to find the source of Hoarse Harold's caltrops, and here it turned out that the *MacIan* smith was willing to make them?

She made a mental note to visit the man and see if he'd sold any to the highwayman.

The *other* highwayman.

They worked in silence for a few moments more, before Allison sighed again, her eyes still closed. "Aye, 'tis a rough price, but worth it to be thought beautiful by one's husband. And while pregnancy has its trials, 'tis worth the joy of kenning ye're bearing yer husband's heir. When ye marry, ye'll understand this, Skye."

Frowning, Skye focused on grabbing a particularly wily hair. This wasn't the first time her sister-in-law had hinted about Skye's marriage, and 'twas likely only a matter of time before she approached Stewart about making an alliance with another clan. If Allison had her way, likely a clan far away.

But…

But Skye was *needed* here on MacIan land. 'Twas only thanks to her and her men that the clan hadn't fallen into debt thus far. And although she and Fiona now lived apart, the idea of being even farther away made her stomach churn.

As did the thought of marriage.

Belonging to a man? Her only purpose to bear him heirs? Her only meaningful attributes her appearance?

His hands on yer body. His lips on yers. His cock in—

Swallowing down a sick feeling in her throat, Skye straightened.

She stood, staring down at her sister-in-law, but she wasn't seeing the bushy orange brows, or even the red irritated skin from her work.

Nay, she was thinking about lying with a man.

A man who wasn't *Duncan Oliphant.*

And was honest enough with herself to admit *that* was the reason she was feeling sick to her stomach.

Unconsciously, her free hand crept to the base of her neck where his ring dangled from a strip of crimson silk. When she and her men had snuck back into the MacIan keep—as easy as always—she'd considered transferring it to a chain. But ultimately, the silk reminded her of her adventure with him, and she'd kept it.

Kept it *and* the ring, which he'd made.

Sometimes at night, in the big empty bed she'd once shared with Fiona, she would pull the ring from under her chemise and slip it over her finger. 'Twas obviously made for a woman, and it fit Skye's third finger perfectly. She wondered if she could still hold a blade with it on.

And then she cursed herself for the thought.

The ring wasn't for her to wear! 'Twas for her to sell and support her clan!

So why hadn't she?

"Skye?" Allison peeked open one eye. "I appreciate ye giving me time to recover, but I am well enough for ye to continue."

Typical Allison, assuming everything was about her.

Stifling a sigh, because she knew irritating her sister-in-law would only create headaches for the rest of the clan, Skye nodded and leaned down again.

But the knock at the door had her snapping upright.

"Skye!"

She recognized Fergus's voice as he pushed the door open and burst in.

Three things happened at once.

One, Skye blurted, "What's amiss?" as she tossed the tweezers into the basin beside her.

Two, the dear older man skidded to a stop, likely in horror, as he took in the sight of Allison in a robe, and half her brows all red and inflamed.

Three, Allison screeched and grabbed the wet cloth, pulling it up and over her face, in an attempt to hide herself.

Of course, *that* meant she knocked over the basin of water, which drenched her entire left side. *And* then, the soaked cloth was sucked inside her mouth when she inhaled to scream again, so her second screech came out as a sort of wet gurgling sound.

Deciding 'twould be wrong to allow her sister-in-law to drown in her bedroom, Skye reached over and pulled the soaked cloth from Allison's mouth, while keeping her attention on her man.

"Fergus, what's amiss?" she repeated, hoping her calm tone belied her nervousness.

"Skye— Milady, I mean."

He offered her a quick bow, which she waved away. They'd never bothered with such formalities.

"Is aught wrong? Is it Bean?" The old man knew her fondness for the gentle giant, and that was the only reason she could imagine him fetching her.

But Allison had finally gotten her breath back. *"What do ye think ye're doing? Bursting in on me like this!"* She still held the cloth, but now she pushed herself ponderously to her feet, shaking her fist at Fergus. "How *dare* ye think to interrupt the laird's wife in the middle of her toilette! I'll have ye flogged for this!"

As Fergus paled—likely from the full sight of Allison riled up, rather than her threat—Skye rolled her eyes.

" 'Tis *my* room, Allison," she reminded her sister-in-law.

Who promptly whirled on her, the wet cloth slapping hither and yon, as she waved it in her clenched fist. "And that makes it *better*? Is this a *normal* occasion?" Her pitch rose with each question. "To have *crofters* and *peasants* coming into yer room during yer toilette? Calling ye by yer given name?" With a gasp, she slapped the cloth to her chest. "What would yer *brother* say?"

Her theatrics were simply adorable.

"Sit down afore ye stress the bairn," Skye snapped. "Fergus is nae crofter; he works in the stables. If ye kenned more about yer new clan, ye'd ken that. He's likely here with a question about my horse."

"Ye have a horse?"

She really didn't know *anything*, did she?

With a sigh, Skye turned back to the door and planted her hands on her hips. "Aye, Fergus? Forgive *Lady Allison's* outburst. She's breeding, ye ken."

Bless him, but the dear old man glanced down at Allison's protruding stomach, then slammed his eyes upward. "Anyone with two brain cells can *tarting* tell that, milady."

His cheeks were pinking under his beard.

"Is my horse aright?"

He kept his attention locked firmly on the ceiling. "Aye—nay. I mean, aye, he's fine. 'Tisnae why I came to fetch ye."

Fetch her?

Frowning slightly now, Skye stepped toward the door, instinctively checking her dagger was in place at her belt.

"Is aught amiss?" she repeated, this time in a near-whisper.

"Ye have a visitor, milady." Fergus must've thought the joists of the ceiling were the most intriguing thing he'd seen all day. "He's asked to see the laird, but as soon as I recognized him, I ran *figtart* to warn ye."

Warn me?

When he finally dropped his eyes to hers, she realized she must've repeated the words aloud. And the fear in his gaze terrified her.

"Fergus?" she whispered, her heart now slamming against the inside of her chest. "Who is it?"

He swallowed once. "Duncan Oliphant. He's come to see yer brother."

Oh, figtart!

CHAPTER 7

FIGTART, figtart, figtart!

Skye likely showed more than a few MacIans her ankles—and possibly her knees—as she ran through the keep, but she was past caring. They all knew she was a little strange, and at that moment, all she cared about was getting to Duncan before he found her brother.

Was he here to tattle on her?

And once he told Stewart what she'd been up to these last months, what would Stewart do? Would she be able to explain her reasons, point out the necessary money she'd brought the clan? Or would he punish her outright?

Better not to even reach that point.

Better to stop Duncan altogether, *before* he could tell Stewart about her highwaymanning.

Highwaywomaning.

Wait, was that even a verb? Could she just *verb* something by using it thus— Wait, wasn't *verb* a verb in that context?

Focus!

Hoisting her skirts up even higher, she fairly flew down the steps to the great hall, praying Duncan was still there.

He was.

He was still there, and he was standing at the base of the stairs, his hands gripping a scabbarded sword in front of him, staring at the cold hearth nearby.

Skye discovered this a little too late, seeing as how she slammed into him, unable to stop her forward momentum.

They might've both tumbled to the ground, but Duncan Oliphant was too well-built for that. Instead, he merely grunted, flexed his knees, then whirled about, grabbing her by the shoulders. Vaguely, she recognized the clatter of the sword he'd been holding as it hit the ground, but then she wasn't thinking much at all. Because he might've thought her a threat at first, but the way he pulled her to his chest, holding her a moment longer than necessary, told him all she needed to know.

Maybe he dinnae come to betray me to Stewart.

Breathless—and she suspected it wasn't just from the run—Skye tilted her head back to look up into his face.

"Why— What are ye doing here, Dunc?"

His grin flashed quickly, and when he spoke, that gravelly voice of his made her thighs clench.

"Do I need a reason to see ye?"

She blinked. "Well…*aye*. Ye came this far just to—to see me?"

"That, and ye have something I want."

Pushing away from him, she stepped out of his arms—and refused to acknowledge the little spike of disappointment the movement caused—and lifted her fingers to the gold ring on the silk ribbon, hidden under her gown.

Clearly, he'd realized she'd forgotten to return it—*forgotten? More like ye just couldnae bear to part with something his fingers had caressed* —and had come to MacIan land to retrieve it.

But why would he need to speak with Stewart?

She swallowed. "Are ye planning to tell my brother?"

"About what?"

She noticed his lips twitch. Was he laughing at her?

Taking a deep breath, she lifted her chin and prayed no one else was listening. "About what I took from ye? About my…hobby…?"

"A hobby, hmm?"

He *was* toying with her!

Her jaw clenched, and Skye felt torn between anger and desperation. "Dinnae be cruel! Just tell me if ye're here to ruin my life or no'!"

This time, a sound burst from his lips, which might've been a chuckle. " 'Tis a bit melodramatic, do ye no' think?"

Oh, God help me!

Her heart pounding in fear, she reached toward him in supplication. But her pride jerked her back, and she ended up taking a stumbling half-step before catching herself.

Angry at the terror she felt and the control this man had over her life, Skye tore at the neckline of her gown, scrambling for the silk ribbon.

"Here. *Here!* Ye came for the damnable ring? I'll give it to ye then, and ye can damned well be on yer way to leave me in peace—"

"Hold, Skye." He lifted his hand, his callused fingertips touching the back of her wrist and freezing her frantic movements.

It was a little embarrassing how her breath caught, her eyes widened, and her chest tightened.

In hope?

She said naught, but held her breath as she waited for him to continue.

He sighed and dropped his hand from her skin. It wasn't until it was gone, she realized how much his touch had felt like a brand.

A kind of brand she *liked*.

"Skye, I dinnae come to cause ye pain." Bending, he scooped up the sword and scabbard he'd dropped. When he straightened, he glanced around, then stepped away to drop the sheathed weapon on one of the tables nearby.

Why?

But then, she suddenly didn't care, because he'd reached out a hand to her in invitation. "Will ye go for a ride with me?"

"A…ride?" she repeated dumbly.

He nodded. "I'd like to speak with ye and—".

"Aye!" she blurted, then took a breath. "I mean, I'd like the chance to speak with ye as well."

And possibly, the chance to do *more*.

Like riding him *mayhap*?

Snorting at her naughty subconscious, Skye shyly placed her hand in his, and didn't even bother to hide the shiver of warmth—and anticipation—which crawled up her arm and lodged in her breasts.

Was this her one opportunity—alone with Duncan, *before* he tells Stewart what she'd been doing—to mayhap change his mind? Was this her one and only chance to save her clan?

And a chance to *kiss* him again…?

DUNCAN AND SKYE'S horses picked their way along a little-used path through a field of wildflowers. He had no idea what kind they were, but the colorful sprays rose above the horse's knees, and each delicate stalk swayed in the slightest of breezes.

Duncan had never thought himself a particular lover of nature, but even he had to admit the MacIan land was beautiful…or perhaps it was the woman within his view which made it so breathtaking.

Skye was just ahead of him, and he was content to follow and admire the way she held herself competently in the saddle.

Her hair was bound up in braids this time, but he could well remember what it had looked—and felt and smelled—like, only a sennight before, when she'd sat proudly in his arms. And there was naught to block his eyes from admiring the way her waist flared down to her tantalizing hips.

St. Simon's head lice!

'Twas impossible not to remember how those hips had felt under his palms, or how *she* had felt, pressed against him.

Which, of course, made him remember the feel of her hands around his cock, and *that* memory sure wasn't going to help matters.

He'd come here to MacIan land to propose a marriage alliance. He'd intended to discuss it with her brother, the laird, first. But the moment she'd barreled into his back, he'd realized he needed *her* approval first.

Skye was the one who mattered.

Ye need to tell her how ye feel about her.

The problem was, he wasn't sure if he could put into words the exact way he felt.

He liked her, aye. He enjoyed being around her. He enjoyed touching her, for certes.

Was that love? Was that enough to propose marriage?

And would she agree?

Did she even feel the same for *him*?

He growled at himself, at the stupid way his thoughts were chasing themselves around his head.

The low rumble he released was louder than he'd intended, and Skye turned in the saddle to raise her brows at him. "Did ye say something?"

Nay.

"Aye," he blurted. "I said, let's stop here."

She pulled her horse to a stop and looked around. They were completely alone in the middle of a little valley, the wildflowers blanketing a vast distance in all directions.

"Here?"

Duncan winced. Knowing him, once he started talking, he'd *have* to touch her, and then where would that leave them? Stuck out here, with their horses wandering around aimlessly?

"Let's head for that big oak." They could tie their animals there.

She waited for him to lead, and when he reached the tree, Duncan swung down from the saddle and looped his reins loosely around a branch.

There. The horse can still graze, and I can—

The thought—and his breath—fled as he watched her dismount. She was competent and sure, aye, but her movements revealed one stocking-covered calf, and he couldn't help but think how those legs would feel wrapped around *him*.

The kind of woman who took a man's cock in her hands, stroking him until he embarrassed himself all over the inside of his kilt, would *not* shy away from wrapping her legs around the man she loved.

Love.

There was that word again.

He watched her take a deep breath and step away from the horses, squaring her shoulders as she met his eyes.

"Aright, Duncan. Here I am. Here *ye* are. Ye said ye wanted the chance to talk to me, so let us talk."

Talk?

What he was imagining—what he had *been* imagining all these days—hadn't included using their tongues for *talking.*

But he cleared his throat, knowing he did indeed need to speak to her. "Skye, I needed to see ye again."

By St. Simon's big toe, ye sound pitiful!

He grimaced and shoved his thumbs into his belt, shifting his weight, as he worked up the bollocks to tell her how he felt.

"Why are ye here, Dunc?"

Well, that was simple enough.

"I owe ye something."

Her lovely blue eyes widened, and her hand flew to her chest. Her fingertips pressed against something hidden under the neckline of her gown, and he remembered the way she'd earlier reached for whatever was hidden there.

"*Ye* owe *me? Something?*" she repeated, then shook her head. "I—I think ye have that backward."

It was her breathlessness, the way she sounded unsure, which bolstered Duncan's courage, more than anything else.

Skye MacIan was *not* hesitant. She was wild and adventurous, and if *she* were unsure, then it was up to *him* to be the one with all the confidence.

He took a step closer to her. "I owe ye a kiss."

The way her head snapped back, and her nostrils flared, told him he'd surprised her, and he felt his lips tug up on one side as he took another step.

Her lips formed the words, "*A kiss?*" but she didn't speak them.

"In fact..."—he lowered his voice, holding her gaze—"I owe ye more than that."

"*Owe?*" She sounded as if she were choking.

Another step, and now he was standing right in front of her. "Do ye ken I had to scrub my own kilt? I had to borrow one of Finn's plaids while it dried."

Her beautiful lips formed a little "*oh*" of surprise. Then she shook her head, and her eyelids lowered as she peeked up at him, a blush staining her cheeks. "*That* kind of owe," she finally said wryly.

He'd made the impulsively wild MacIan sister blush?

Excellent.

She made his heart swell.

Well, his heart and *other things.*

Lifting one hand, he brushed the backs of his fingers across her cheek. And when her lids fluttered and she leaned into his touch, he turned his hand around to cup her face.

"Will ye let me repay ye, lass?" he whispered, wondering if those words were enough to convey exactly what he wanted.

When she opened her eyes to meet his gaze, she didn't pull away from his touch.

"I've thought of it," she said simply.

He swallowed.

It?

Did she understand what he was asking?

I want to love ye, Skye MacIan. I want to bring ye joy, pleasure and ecstasy. Let me repay ye.

But why the *fook* couldn't he just say those very words aloud?

Mayhap she'd heard them anyway, because she straightened, and his hand slid down to cup the back of her neck, holding her, because to *not* hold her in this moment would be impossible.

"Duncan..." Her tongue flicked out over her lower lip, a surprisingly arousing sign of hesitation. "I've thought of *ye.* When I touch myself, I imagine 'tis *yer* hands on me. Yer lips. Yer—"

Her words had struck him mute, but his breath burst from his lips in a desperate groan, and he pulled her tight against his chest.

She was tucked against him, his hand splayed across her back, holding her safe, and her words echoing in his ears.

I imagine 'tis yer hands on me.

His hand shook as he slowly began pulling the pins from her hair, letting it cascade down and fall loosely around her shoulders.

St. Simon's beard, but her locks felt silkier than anything he'd ever touched before, and likely anything he'll ever touch in the future.

I imagine 'tis yer hands on me.

Touching her hair—although he'd ached to do so for much too long—wasn't enough. He needed to touch *her*.

I imagine 'tis yer hands on me.

It took two tries to get his throat working again. "Let me," he finally managed hoarsely.

Her voice was muffled, pressed against his chest, but he *felt* her words. "Aye. *Please.*"

CHAPTER 8

FROM WHAT LITTLE he knew of anatomy—most of his learning having come from Malcolm's ramblings—Duncan knew his heart hadn't *actually* stopped, but it had felt that way when she reached up and pulled his head down to hers.

Their lips met in a sort of desperation he could only describe as necessity.

In that moment, it was *vital* he kiss her, taste her. The idea of doing aught else was inconceivable.

When she moaned against his lips, he was lost.

Duncan lifted her easily in order to trail his lips down her cheek and jaw. And when she dropped her head back and made a little desperate sound, his kisses flowed down her neck to the soft spot behind her ear.

She was tugging at his shirt and pulling at the plaid he'd draped over his shoulder. When he lowered her and loosened his hold on her, she stumbled back, and for a moment, his heart dropped into his stomach with the realization he might've been forcing his attentions where they weren't wanted.

Skye stood, wide-eyed and panting, staring at him. While her breasts heaved under their silk confines, she lifted trembling fingertips to her lips, and he wondered how in damnation he was going to apologize.

But then...

Then she reached for the ties holding her gown shut, fingers trembling, yet hurrying, and he jumped forward to help her.

In moments, her gown was unlaced, and *she* was the one to push it from her shoulders, with an erotic little noise of desperate need.

And he saw it.

There, hanging atop her linen chemise, was his ring. The very same one he'd used as an excuse to invite himself to MacIan land. She was wearing the small metal piece around her neck on a strip of red ribbon, and it dangled alluringly between her breasts.

It was his; he'd made it, and she wore it.

She was *his*.

With a groan, he reached for her, not caring she hadn't had the time to even push the material down her arms yet. Nay, all he could see was her voluptuously glorious tits, teasing him behind their translucent layer of fine linen.

One of his hands pressed against her left breast, and Duncan was careful not to squeeze as tightly as he wanted to. But when she sucked in a breath and thrust the orb harder against his palm, his gaze snapped up to hers.

She was chewing on her lower lip, searching his eyes for...something.

"Skye?" He knew his voice was hoarse, but—*St. Simon help him!*—it was damn near impossible to rein in the desire coursing through his blood, not to mention his cock, at that moment.

When she released her lip, it had become redder and plumper, and captured his fascinated gaze.

"Duncan..."

She whispered his name, and when he lifted his eyes to hers, he saw the need there.

"I want ye." This time there was no denying her words. "*Please*."

He didn't hesitate any longer to pull the linen chemise from her shoulders, then close both hands around her breasts. While the pad of one of his callused thumbs played with one nipple, he nudged the dangling ring out of the way and lowered his tongue to the other. Her little whimper of approval was almost as good as the way she thrust her pelvis forward, so fast, they both almost lost their balance.

God Almighty, but he *wanted* her!

Any more of this though, and they'd fall over and hurt themselves. He'd love to see how they tried to explain their injuries to her brother.

Although it damn near killed him, he stepped away long enough to fumble with his belt and undo his kilt. As he kicked off his boots, he shook the plaid out and laid it on the ground, crushing enough of the wildflowers to fill the air with their scent.

When he turned to reach for her again, she'd already pulled her gown and chemise down over her hips, letting them drop to the ground in a pile of color and satin, and had removed her slippers. She stood there, breathing fast, in naught but her stockings and his ring on the ribbon around her neck.

Duncan was certain he'd never seen anything more beautiful.

He held molten metal on a daily basis. He'd burned himself more times than he could count. The skin of his hands was tough and callused, but he couldn't stop his hands from trembling slightly as he reached for her hair, then skimmed his fingers through the silky softness.

"Skye," he whispered, knowing his voice was shaking, "I dinnae ken if I can be as gentle as ye need—"

She silenced him by lifting herself on her toes and pushing her lips against his. With a groan, his arms went around her back, pulling her flush against him. All that stood between them now was the thin layer of his shirt, which did naught to block the hardness of his cock currently pressing into her stomach.

With a gasp, she broke their kiss, then pushed hard against his shoulders. "Take this off! Lie down on that plaid, Dunc! *Hurry.*"

Despite the haze of desire clouding his mind, his brows rose at her commands. "Lass, are ye sure—"

Skye growled an impatient curse, then dropped to the plaid

herself, before pulling on his hand to signal she wanted him to join her on the pitiful bed he'd made for them. "If I'd wanted a man who would treat me like a wee delicate creature, Duncan Oliphant, I wouldnae have fallen in love with *ye*. Now *hurry!*"

Her words registered instantly and caused his heart to slam against the inside of his chest, in a way even his arousal hadn't. But by her actions, he doubted she'd even realized what she'd claimed.

Fallen in love with ye.

Did she...?

Could she...?

Duncan shook his head and sunk to his knees on the kilt beside her. "Lass, I..."

"Take off yer shirt," she commanded.

Well, he couldn't argue with that.

His mind still on her casual—*accidental?*—admission, Duncan fumbled with the bottom of his shirt, pulling it up and over his head. When he emerged, he did his best to hold on to his current thought.

"Lass, did ye just—"

But she wasn't listening, nay. In fact, she wasn't paying his words *any* attention. Instead, she was staring at his cock, which stood out from its nest of curls much like some kind of hungry beast.

Did ye just compare yer wee willy to a hungry beast?

Shut up.

He tried again. "Skye, I came to see yer brother because—"

Apparently, she was done talking.

Eyes wide, she reached for him, curling her fingers around his shaft, in a way which made him suck in a startled, yet thrilled, breath.

Kneeling on his kilt, he found himself thrusting his hips toward her, desperate for more of her touch.

"Oh, Duncan," she murmured, her gaze riveted on his member, " 'tis so hard...yet soft too. *Feeling* 'tis so different from just seeing it, ye ken?"

She was examining him as Malcolm might study a new insect he'd discovered.

Then her eyes snapped up to his. "Can I taste it?"

He wanted to think he'd said something smooth and appealing, but Duncan suspected the noise which escaped his lips was more like a, "*Whaag?*"

But that appeared to be the only encouragement she needed, because Skye leaned forward and dragged her tongue across the tip of his cock, and all coherent thoughts he may have once had were long gone.

Duncan tipped his head back, squinting up at the impossibly blue sky, and wondered what piece of saintly work he'd done to deserve this.

Ye came here to tell her ye love her! To propose marriage!

Aye, aye, and he *would*…just as soon as he…

Ahh!

Her lips had closed around his shaft, and she'd pulled him deep into her warm, wet mouth.

Wait, what had he been thinking about?

One of her hands fell to his bollocks, while the other inched around to cup his arse. St. Simon's tits, but it felt divine!

And then her tongue slid along his shaft, and he jerked forward. She made a little noise—he couldn't tell if it was surprise or pleasure—and he cursed.

Pulling from her mouth was one of the hardest things he'd ever done, but he forced himself to drop back on his heels and sink to the ground, his breathing heavy and uneven.

"*Skye*! I cannae— If ye keep doing that, I'll no' last!"

In response, she cupped her palms around her tits and squeezed, then dropped her head back with a moan, and he gave up.

He'd come here to make her his, and this seemed like the most enjoyable way.

In a blink, he was beside her, placing his hand over hers, squeezing, as he lowered his head to suckle. With his hand, he supported her head as he laid her back on the plaid, so she was stretched out before him like a buffet.

His lips trailed across her tits to her belly, then lower. Her hand had dropped to her curls, and she was touching herself, the way she'd done against the tree the morning he'd pinned her, and she'd taken control of his body and heart so thoroughly.

When I touch myself, I imagine 'tis yer hands on my body.

Against the skin of her navel, he grinned.

Well, ye dinnae have to imagine any longer, lass.

When his lips reached her curls, her thighs parted, dropping apart willingly. He kissed the smooth skin at the inside of one thigh, his nose filled with her musky, perfect scent.

And when he dragged his tongue up her wet slit, her arse bucked off the ground violently.

He lifted his head just long enough to blow across her sensitive bud, and say in a soothing tone, "Shh, lass. Let me love ye."

In response, she moaned and seemed to melt into the ground, so he took her reaction as approval and lowered his lips to her core once more. This time though, he used the pad of his thumb against the nub of her pleasure, as he slid first one finger, then two, inside her heated inner core.

Was she even aware of how her hips gyrated under his ministrations? Did she hear the erotic little mewls of pleasure she was making?

And then he felt her muscles tightening around his fingers, and knew she was ready. He dragged one palm up the inside of her thigh as he closed his lips around the pearl hidden within her soft brown curls...and grinned in satisfaction as she found her release.

"*Dunc!*" Skye cried hoarsely, her stomach muscles tightening so intensely, she almost sat up involuntarily as she pulsed around his fingers.

She was panting as hard as he was, and he knew he was in danger of ruining *another* plaid,, if he spilled atop this one.

But he desperately needed to be inside her.

Surging up to his knees, he planted his weight on one palm on the ground near her head, and before she'd even fully relaxed from her orgasm, he caught her gaze. "Skye..."

Her chest was still heaving, but she reached up and placed her hands on his upper arms, tugging at him. *"Please*, Duncan...stop teasing me and make me *yers!"*

St. Simon, could she tempt him any further?

He squeezed his eyes shut and tried to breathe—and *think*—normally. "Skye, I cannae," he managed. "I came here to tell ye something."

I love ye.

Why could he no' just blurt it out?

Marry me, lass.

Why were those words so hard?

Because every single drop of blood no' currently keeping ye alive, is making yer cock too hard to think.

Ah. Well, 'twas an explanation at least.

And then, to his surprise, he felt her ankle hook around the back of his thigh, pulling him forward. He might've kept his balance, except the other leg joined the first, and her legs were then around him, tight, and yanking him forward.

Giving up the fight, he reached for his cock to guide it to her entrance.

I should've told her I loved her first.

SKYE KNEW she wasn't thinking coherently, but that was aright. She'd just experienced the most intense climax of her life, and that was just from Duncan's *tongue.* She couldn't even imagine what his *cock* would feel like!

Luckily, she wouldn't have to imagine long, because she knew what she wanted, and would make damn sure she got it.

As she lifted her arse cheeks off the plaid, she briefly wondered what he'd intended to tell her that day. Mayhap something about—

Oh!

When he entered her, she couldn't help the way she froze, the stretching sensation more than she'd expected. He was a big man—

big all over—and while she was no wilting violet, she still needed a moment to adjust.

"Skye? Love?"

As always, his low growl sent her stomach fluttering. Only this time, she suspected it had to do with a *lot* more than his voice.

It wasn't until she opened her eyes, she realized she'd closed them. He held himself still, supporting himself on his hands, planted on either side of her.

She swallowed and forced herself to exhale, to relax. Her hands were still on his upper arms, and now she slid her palms along his skin, reaching his shoulders, and then his neck, in a loving caress.

"Are ye in pain, love?"

The concern in his voice did more to alleviate her discomfort than anything else. That, and the knowledge he'd waited, had remained frozen in place, when it was clear he'd much rather be moving. She could *feel* the coiled tension in his shoulders and body.

Slowly, she inhaled and exhaled again, allowing her body to adjust to his. Then she tightened her legs around his hips.

That must've been the only encouragement he'd needed, because with a wicked little twitch of his brow, he flexed his pelvis in one swift movement, pushing into her fully, before retreating just slightly.

Inhaling sharply through her nose, her eyes widened.

That had felt…*good.*

Delightful even.

Almost as good as she'd hoped.

But how could it compare to the release she'd just experienced?

Intrigued, but also not certain she was ready to commit further, Skye cast about for something to say.

What had he mentioned?

Oh, aye.

"Ye said ye—"

Before the words were even out of her mouth, he flexed again, driving his thick member into her deeply, then out again.

How could such a slight movement cause her insides to go all squishy?

He was watching her intently, as if he were interested in what she'd been saying.

"Ye had something to ask—"

This time she bit off her words with a gasp, because he'd pulled almost all the way out of her, then slid back in, and—*Blessed Virgin*—but that had felt wonderful.

"Again!" she rasped.

With a grin, he did.

And then again, and a third time. By the fourth time, he'd dropped his chin to his chest with a groan, and was no longer looking at her.

And God forgive her, but *watching* him in the throes of pleasure was almost as arousing as the way he was making her feel physically.

The veins in his neck stood out, as if he were holding himself under tight rein. And the careful, controlled thrusts he was making *felt* nice, for certes, but there was something in his movement which hinted at much more.

"Duncan," she finally gasped, and when his gaze snapped up, she licked her lips. "Ye said— *Oh God!*" He was watching her, but hadn't halted his careful strokes, in and out of her wetness. "Ye said ye'd come to ask me— *Duncan!*"

"Ye like that, lass?"

Unbidden, her legs tightened around his hips. "Ye ken I do. Do it again." This time, the strength of his thrust pushed her arse into the ground. "Aye, please!"

Once more, then a pained look showed in his eyes. "I cannae hurt ye, love."

Her fingernails dug into the skin on the backs of his shoulders. "Ye could nae hurt me. Please…!"

She wasn't even sure what she was pleading for. All she knew was, the pressure was building inside her again, and she hated the idea of him keeping control, when *she* couldn't.

Not when it came to him and the way he made her feel.

"Lass," he began, but she used her grip on him to pull him forward, to silence his protests with her lips.

And that was all the encouragement he needed.

He growled against her mouth, then clasped one hand to her hip and rolled, taking her with him. Suddenly, she found herself straddling him, her knees on either side of his hips.

Unwilling to remain plastered against him, she pushed herself upright, mimicking his pose from a moment ago. The ring on its silk ribbon swung between her breasts. Just as she opened her mouth to ask what she needed to do, he settled his hands on her hips.

"Hold yer weight, love," he commanded.

When he planted his heels and thrust upward, settling deeply inside her, Skye's eyes widened at the sensation. This was different from before, but just as perfect. She lowered her head, braced her weight on her hands, and spread her knees even farther, as he slammed upward, again and again.

It was *magnificent*.

In moments, unwilling to remain passive, she was rocking back and forth atop him, meeting him thrust for thrust. The pressure had built to an almost unbearable level, and she began panting, with her eyes squeezed shut and her lips open.

Was he enjoying himself as much as she was?

As soon as she could wrench her attention away from the glorious friction he was creating within her, she'd ask him. Just as soon as—

What had they been saying?

"Lass," he panted, "I think…I should…tell ye…"

His words were punctuated by his thrusts, and she groaned with pleasure, tilting her head to one side.

"Aye?" she managed, forcing her eyes open.

"The reason…I came here— *St. Simon, bless me!*"

He was so close. She could *feel* him swelling within her, the way he'd swelled in her hand that morning in the woods. Keeping her gaze on him, she marveled *she* had the power to do this to him.

The knowledge she'd brought him to pleasure once again was enough to cause her inner muscles to clench tightly, and he groaned.

"Marry me, Skye," he rasped, his eyes flying open. "Be my wife."

Her eyes widened. "*What!*"

But he hadn't stilled. Instead, he reached between their joined bodies and dragged his callused thumb across her bud. The sensation was more than she could ignore, and with a shudder, her climax burst over her.

Skye's limbs seemed to liquify, but he kept the steady pressure on the point of her pleasure as he grabbed her hip with his other hand and drove into her once, twice, thrice!

And then, with a roar, he thrust upward and held the position. Vaguely, through her own release, she felt warmth flooding her womb, and in that moment, Skye knew Duncan had made her his.

Despite the shock of his question, she couldn't deny the perfection of the feeling.

CHAPTER 9

STILL BREATHING HEAVILY, Duncan untangled his arms, but only just long enough to wrap them around her and draw her close. He was still lodged inside her and was unwilling to lose their connection so soon.

Taking it as a good sign when she willingly tucked her head under his chin and pressed her cheek to his chest, he concentrated on controlling his body's reaction to her.

St. Simon's left bollock, but she'd bewitched him!

Skye MacIan was wild and willful and wonderful, and she did something to his heart and body he couldn't deny.

"I love ye," he whispered, brushing his lips across her shoulder.

She stiffened at his words, but at least she didn't pull away when she said against his skin, " 'Tis a hell of a time to admit that."

He couldn't help his smile, knowing what she meant. "I'm no' just saying that because of the mind-altering sex we just had."

She was quiet for a moment, then hummed. "Mind-altering, eh?"

He *could* make a joke, but instead, told her, "Being with ye is what being in Heaven must feel like, lass."

When she straightened her arms and pushed herself up off his chest, his softening member slid from her, and they both winced. She didn't speak, but just stared down at him.

"Skye?"

"I think that is the most wonderful thing anyone has ever said to me, Dunc," she said in a serious tone.

He matched the sincerity, when he replied, " 'Tis true. 'Tis why I journeyed to MacIan land."

"To tell me I'm Heavenly?"

He dragged a hand down her back to rest on her hip and resisted the urge to make a quip about her *heavenly body*. "To tell ye I love ye."

Her blue eyes narrowed. "And ye want me to be yer wife?"

It was her tone which had him wincing. "Ach, well, I was going to ask yer brother for yer hand, before I realized *ye* were the one whose approval I needed most." Hopeful, he smiled up at her. "*Will* ye be mine, Skye?"

"Because ye need a wife? Because yer father says ye must marry?"

It wasn't the response he'd expected when he proposed marriage to a woman.

Of course, he'd never actually *expected* to be proposing marriage to a woman, so what in damnation did *he* know?

And...she was still waiting for an answer.

He swallowed, suddenly wishing he wasn't so distracted by her naked tits dangling right above his mouth.

"I..." He shook his head. "Da's demand took me by surprise, I'll admit. I didnae intend on complying, because I have nae interest in being a laird."

"And *I* have nae interest in being a laird's wife."

With a little scoff, she swung one leg over him, kneeling at his side, as the ring swung on its ribbon against her skin. He nearly groaned in disappointment when her body left his, but was pleased again when she leaned against his hip, obviously not ready to abandon him altogether.

Before he could reply to her bold statement, she pulled her hair over one shoulder and began to braid it in what looked to be a nervous gesture. "Ye said ye wanted a wife who would be content with only ye, remember? A little cottage beside yer forge?"

How could he forget? He'd fallen asleep that night believing she wouldn't share a life such as that with him.

Now, with his heart in his throat, he croaked, "Aye. I said if I married, I wanted a wife who could share that life with me. I'm no' ready to be a father, no' if it means a clan's responsibilities are to be thrust upon my shoulders."

She hummed, and her gaze drifted to the tree behind his head where the horses were still tethered.

"I have nae objection to children in general, but I never saw much need for them in *my* life."

Slowly, Duncan blew out a controlled breath.

Was she...*agreeing* with him?

"Skye, love..." How to say it? "I ken ye have nae reason to love me." Still, he couldn't forget her casual admission, as she'd pulled him down to the plaid. "And that night, when I held ye as ye slept, I thought..."

By St. Simon's elbow, was it *always* going to be this hard to discuss his feelings?

Shaking his head, he pushed himself upright, shivering a little as a cool summer breeze swept over his skin, still slick with sweat from their lovemaking.

"Ye thought *what?*" Skye pushed.

With a muttered curse, he dragged his fingers through his hair and propped one elbow on the knee he'd dragged forward. She'd straightened as he sat up, and had shifted, until she now sat cross-legged beside him, her fingers still trying to tame her hair.

Her eyes were on him, but Duncan figured it would be easier to have a deeper conversation if he weren't looking at her, so he focused on the sway of the wildflowers in the gentle breeze.

"I thought..." He swallowed again. "I thought I wanted a biddable wife. One who'd be content with *me*. I thought a lass like ye—ye're a *highwayman*, for fook's sake!—was too wild and impulsive to be happy with someone as boring as myself."

He paused, hoping she'd deny his words, or even acknowledge

them if it was the truth. But when she remained silent, he realized he was going to have to ask her directly.

So he braced himself, then forced himself to meet her eyes. "I realized I wasnae giving ye enough credit. Since that morning in the stables at my father's keep, I've thought of little else besides ye. Even after ye punched me for kissing ye again, I was enamored. My brothers teased me, but I couldnae stop the way my heart sped up when ye were around. 'Twas why I kenned I needed to leave Oliphant Castle while ye were still there, because ye had nae reason to think kindly of me."

She'd finished her braid, but continued to hold the end of it in one hand. "I saw ye standing proudly with yer kilt up around yer ears in front of all of Creation, Dunc. I promise ye, I was *no'* the only woman who had reason to think kindly of ye."

His lips pulled into a reluctant smile, knowing she was teasing him.

"My point is…" With a sudden lunge, afraid if he hesitated, he'd lose the bollocks, he snatched her hands away from her hair and squeezed them. "I kenned ye and I didnae belong together, but I was still enamored. And then when I saw ye lying in the road that day…"

He shook his head, still remembering the dread he'd felt. "Well, I still dinnae understand all that went on that day, but I *do* ken I cannae think of aught else than *ye*, Skye MacIan. I didnae intend it, but somewhere along the way, I fell in love with ye. I want ye to be my wife."

And then, when she didn't say a word, he lifted his brows hopefully. "*Please?*"

She didn't pull away, but she did turn her head, though her gaze went straight back to that damnable tree again.

"I think…"

Her voice was so low, he almost didn't hear her, and he was sitting right next to her.

"I think, somewhere along the way, I've fallen in love with ye too, Dunc."

The confirmation of her earlier slip should've made his heart leap, but all he could think about was how...*sad* she looked.

Releasing her hands, he placed one palm against her cheek and turned her gaze back to him. "And why does that confession sound so painful for ye, lass?"

Where those...tears? Her lovely blue eyes were filling with *tears*?

"Because I cannae marry ye. My clan needs me here."

It was a beautiful day. There were birds calling one another, and bloody bees buzzing around the wildflowers, doing whatever the fook bees did. The sun was shining, the breeze was blowing, and he'd just made the most *mind-altering* love of his life, to a woman he wanted to marry.

He'd be *damned* if he were going to let her go without a fight.

"Tell me," he demanded. "Make me understand why ye cannae —*willnae*—be mine."

With a sigh, she pulled away from him, lacing her hands in her lap and staring down at them. She looked more uncomfortable than at any other time he'd seen her.

"My brother's wife, Allison, comes from a small clan; a clan even smaller and less important than mine. She thinks being married to Stewart is some kind of big coup."

"It likely is." He hooked his elbow around his knee to keep from reaching for her. "Although I dinnae ken much about marriage prospect for lasses, being a smith and all."

When she peeked up at him through her lashes, he saw something twinkling in her eyes. "*Goldsmiths* are still considered marital prizes, I believe," she quipped primly.

"Och, aye! I'm a veritable prince."

So why will ye no' marry me?

As if she heard his unspoken words, her shoulders slumped once more. "Well, Allison sees naught wrong with spending all of the MacIan coin. We barely made it through last winter, and that was *with* Fiona's bargaining skills. This spring, it became obvious we wouldnae survive her spending."

"She's frivolous?"

Skye shrugged. "She sees naught wrong with buying velvets we dinnae need, and decorations we cannae afford, in order to make us look fancier than we are."

Frowning, Duncan considered her words. "And yer brother doesnae stop her?"

"*Well*... When Fiona and I brought it up to him, he made it clear he wanted to keep her happy, at all costs, though I dinnae think he truly meant that literally. But regardless, the vile woman gets what she wants." Skye grimaced. "She can be a right harridan if she doesnae get her way."

"So he just *allows* her to waste the clan's money?"

Skye met his eyes sadly. "Love makes one do strange things."

Like sitting buck-arse naked on a plaid in the middle of nature, where anyone could wander by, and no' caring?

He almost snorted in agreement.

"But surely Stewart sees the debt her spending is making for yer clan, does he no'?"

She shook her head, looking resigned. "He's never cared much for ledgers and numbers, and leaves the running of the place to the seneschal. 'Tis how I'm able to sneak into his solar and put in new entries."

Like a flash of lightening, Duncan understood. "The coin ye take from yer robberies. Ye're giving it to yer brother?"

"Nay, I'm giving it to my *clan*. Even with all her spending, the money we're losing isnae accounted for. For a while, I suspected Allison was taking more than she recorded, but I dinnae ken why or how. So I just do the best I can with Fergus and my men, and keep funneling the coin back into the MacIan coffers."

"For Allison to pilfer and waste all over again," he spat out, disgusted by the woman who was giving her sister-in-law no choice but to be a highwayman, all so she could live in luxury the clan couldn't afford.

Skye didn't reply, but didn't deny his words either. She pulled her knees up to her chest and wrapped her arms around her legs. When she propped her chin up on her knees, she appeared forlorn.

Duncan couldn't stand seeing her that way. He shifted closer to her, putting one arm around her shoulders, and pulling her close. They were still nude, aye, but the sun was warm, and despite the seriousness of their conversation, he still felt the languidness which came after a sexual release.

With her head pillowed against his chest, he inhaled, smelling the leather-and-pear scent, which was uniquely Skye, and knew he wasn't going to give up on her.

"Thank ye for explaining why ye turned highwayman, Skye," he murmured, knowing she'd be able to feel his words, as much as hear them.

And he smiled when she primly corrected, "Highway*woman*."

"Yer clan needs money, and ye feel responsible. Well, my offer comes with a bride price, thanks to my father's generosity. I hadnae paid much attention to it, because I didnae plan on marrying, even with his edict, but I understand 'tis generous. Yer brother has Fiona's bride price from Finn…if ye agreed to be my wife, he'd have double that."

"And Allison would fritter it away before the year was out, I dinnae doubt." Skye's words were muffled against his chest, but he still heard them. "I need to be here, to find a way to keep bringing in coin, else the clan will suffer."

If he wasn't mistaken, he swore he heard genuine sorrow in her voice. Using his hold on her shoulders and back, he pulled her away just enough to stare down into her eyes.

Aye, those were tears. It *was* sorrow.

"I love ye, Skye," he whispered. "Does that count for naught?"

"That counts for *everything*." She sniffed, forcing a watery smile his way. "And I love ye too. I hadnae planned on falling in love, Dunc, but ye are kind and level-headed and steadfast. I'd be proud to be yer wife…if I could."

Instead of despairing, Duncan's heart leapt at her confession.

She loved him and would marry him *if she could.*

All he had to do was figure out how to make it so she could.

Nay. Nay, 'tis up to Stewart *to figure out how.*

The realization struck Duncan so hard, he sucked in a breath.

Aye, that was it!

" 'Tisnae fair to rest all of the clan's woes and worries about the future on *yer* shoulders," he whispered, his mind whirling with possibilities.

"What?"

Stewart needed to know all of this. *He* was the one who needed to control his wife's pilfering and stop the clan's money woes at the source. He was the *laird*, for fook's sake!

Not Skye.

And once the *laird* took command of his clan—and his wife—then Skye would be free to marry Duncan.

"Come," he said, pulling them both to their feet in one swift movement. The little squeak she made told him she hadn't been ready, but soon they were both standing among the wildflowers.

"What are ye doing?" she gasped, as he scooped up her chemise and gown and tossed them to her.

Shaking out his plaid, he grinned at her. "We're heading back to yer keep. I have an appointment with yer brother." Her eyes widened as he made short work of wrapping the plaid around him. "I'm going to marry ye, Skye MacIan. That's a promise."

CHAPTER 10

Her hair was still a mess, and anyone who looked at her flushed face and disheveled gown, would know *exactly* what she'd been up to, but Skye couldn't bring herself to care.

In the stables, Duncan swung her down from his horse, and his hands lingered at her waist. Although she'd brought her own horse on their little adventure, she'd returned to the MacIan keep sitting on Duncan's lap, her horse following behind, and knew what message that sent to anyone who saw them.

Allison would have a fit when she found out Skye wasn't "*acting as befitting the sister of a great laird.*"

Well, Allison could go suck on a year-old egg for all Skye cared.

Because Duncan wanted to *marry* her, and judging by the determined tilt of his lovely lips, as he took Skye's hand and strode toward the keep, all the Heavenly Saints couldn't keep him from accomplishing his goal.

She lifted her skirts in her other hand and didn't bother hiding her excited grin.

A fortnight ago, she would've said she had no interest in marrying. Just a short time ago, she would've said she was destined to live the rest of her life working for the betterment of the MacIan clan.

But then…she'd come apart in this man's arms, heard him declare his love for her, and now she had hope for a real future, which surprised her.

They slowed when they stepped into the great hall, but he glanced over at her and squeezed her hand. "I love ye, Skye," he reminded her.

And that was enough to make her heart flutter.

"Whatever ye have planned, best have yer words ready." She jerked her chin toward the stairs on the far side of the hall. "My brother's likely in his solar, just up there."

Duncan nodded firmly, but didn't head directly for the stairs. Instead, he stopped to pick up the scabbarded sword he'd left on one of the trestle tables earlier. Had it really only been a few hours ago she'd barreled into him in this room, delighted to see him again, though terrified what his presence meant?

Hefting the scabbard in his left hand, he reached for her once more...but suddenly jerked to a stop. Bean had materialized out of nowhere, looming menacingly over Duncan. Skye's love tilted his head back and scowled up at the giant.

"Get out of my way."

"Want me to hit him, milady?" Bean rumbled.

Before she could say aught, Duncan lifted the sword in his left hand and poked the other man in the chest with the hilt. "I have a gift for ye."

Skye and the giant were both surprised by his declaration. Bean took a step back, blinking in confusion as he glanced at Skye. She shrugged slightly, not knowing what Duncan meant.

"A gift?" Bean repeated, his voice full of suspicion.

"Aye."

Duncan dropped her hand and drew the sword. Both Skye and Bean tensed for his attack, but instead, he flipped the weapon around and offered it to the giant, hilt first.

As Bean hesitated, Duncan said, "I ken 'tisnae my best work, but I also ken ye're without a full blade. Yer sword is broken, and as I was making this one, I thought ye might like a new one."

Slowly, the giant wrapped his hand around the hilt, pulling it from Duncan's grip. It was clear to Skye he was confused by the gift.

Had no one ever given him aught before?

Her fingers rose to the ring she'd tucked back under her gown, clutching the metal through the silk. Duncan had every right to hold a grudge against Bean—and her as well, for that matter—but he'd made the other man a *gift*, and had offered her marriage. He was most definitely a very special man.

Seeing the giant was still confused, Skye spoke around the lump in her throat. "I thought…I thought the sword was yers?"

Duncan shrugged, stepping back and reaching for her hand again. "I need one, aye, since I left mine lying in the road when I was beset by a lovely highwayman." He winked at her. "But I'll have time to work on another one later."

He'd put another's needs before his own, and that told her everything she needed to know about this man she'd fallen in love with.

" 'Tis really for me?" Bean rumbled in confusion.

"Aye, Bean." Duncan's voice was gentle. "Because ye need one."

"Well, then…" The giant shrugged, then switched his hold on the sword. In one motion, he pulled a different sword from his own scabbard and held it out—one blade in each hand, his size dwarfing the weapons—and nodded happily. "Here's yers."

Duncan dropped her hand and lunged forward to snatch his sword from Bean. "Ye saved it!" He beamed down at the blade. "Thank ye, Bean!"

" 'Twas no' mine," the bigger man said with a shrug. Then Bean stepped back and lifted the sword Duncan had made for him. He studied it for a moment, then in one quick movement, snapped the blade over his knee.

Both Duncan and Skye reared back in surprise at the suddenness of it.

But Bean nodded happily and tossed the broken blade over his shoulder, not seeming to notice when it hit another table and bounced off. He held up the short part of the blade, still connected to the hilt, and smiled.

"Perfect!" With a flourish, he slid it into his scabbard and patted it happily.

Pressing her lips together to keep from laughing, Skye cut her eyes toward Duncan. He was staring bug-eyed at the giant, his mouth open wide in surprise.

I could've told him Bean would do that.

But instead of explaining the gentle giant refused to use a blade, she simply reached over and placed one finger under Duncan's chin, closing his mouth.

The nudge seemed to shake him from his shock, and he blinked, then smiled at her. "Well, now that *that's* taken care of, mayhap we could—"

"What's amiss?"

This time, 'twas Fergus who interrupted them, hurrying toward their little group, with Pierre on his heels. Both men gripped the hilts of their swords and eyed Duncan menacingly.

"Peace, Fergus," she said, with a weary sigh. "Ye have nae need to harm Duncan."

Her old retainer switched his glare to her, taking care to sweep his gaze over her sloppy braid and disheveled dress. "That tarting *custard*." he growled.

Hearing the threat in the dessert-filled curse, Duncan tugged her closer, stepping in front of her.

The dear man thought to protect her from Fergus?

She placed her free hand on Duncan's arm. "*Peace*, I said," she repeated to both men. "Naught's amiss. Duncan has asked me to be his wife, and we're going to see Stewart."

Hopefully, Dunc has a good plan to ensure my clan is provided for, so I can leave them without worry.

At her news, Fergus's face lit up. "Ye'll be heading to Oliphant land then?"

"Dinnae look so pleased, auld man," she said with a frown. "I thought ye'd miss me..."

"Lass, I just want ye out of harm's way!" Fergus stepped forward and wrapped her in his arms, and Skye released Duncan long enough to return the hug.

"Fine," she mumbled against his shoulder, "but I'm taking ye with me."

"And me?" Bean rumbled.

"I'd take ye all to Oliphant land if I could." She pulled away with a deep breath, offering a sad smile to her friends. "Ye've been like family to me, and have always answered my calls when I needed ye."

"*Félicitations pour vos fiançailles!*" Pierre slapped Duncan on the shoulder. "*Est-ce à dire que nous avons fini?*"

"I dinnae ken," Bean rumbled with a shrug. "Almond, mayhap. Or blueberry."

Duncan frowned briefly at the big man, before shrugging and turning to Pierre. "*Oui. Certainement. Je m'occuperai de Skye à l'avenir.*"

While Pierre nodded, pleased, Skye gaped at Duncan. "Ye speak French?"

"Aye," he drawled. "Master Claire was born and raised in Paris before she married. I had to learn when I apprenticed with her, else I'd understand little of the skills she was teaching me."

"So all this time…" Skye glanced between Duncan and Pierre. "Ye ken what Pierre's been saying?"

Pierre grinned. "*C'est agréable d'entendre le français parlé par quelqu'un d'autre.*"

And Bean, bless his soul, nodded. "I like apple ones the best too."

Skye pinched the bridge of her nose. Bean had been translating for Pierre all these months, but what had the Frenchman truly been saying?

"Looks like today's the day for visitors," Fergus said under his breath.

All of them turned to see Skye's brother Stewart descending the stairs, a scowl clearly evident on his face. Behind him, Allison—her brows only half-plucked because Skye had run out when she'd gotten news of Duncan's arrival—was being escorted down the stairs by her own brother.

Skye couldn't hold back her own scowl when she saw him. "What's *Harold* doing here?"

Allison's brother Harold was even more of a pain in the arse than *she* was. After his visits, large amounts of gold always went missing from the coffers. Skye had always suspected it either he was stealing it from Allison and Stewart, or the man was whining to his sister to steal it for him.

Even now, the man was dressed above his status in a fine velvet robe, despite the heat of the day. He and Allison were as alike as twins, with their bushy orange brows and frizzy curls.

It wasn't until Duncan glanced her way, that Skye realized she was squeezing his hand tightly and had a look of disgust on her face. So she schooled her features and lowered her voice, so only he could hear. "I dislike that man immensely. He makes rude insinuations, and I suspect he's the root of Allison's pilfering."

Duncan's frown didn't ease. "Why would a monk dress so finely, even to visit his sister?"

"Monk?" He had her full attention now. "Harold is nae monk." Not even *close*, based on the lascivious way he'd looked at her on his last visit.

"Och, aye," Duncan jerked his chin at the orange-haired couple, who were speaking with their heads together as they walked. "I traveled with him on the road from Eriboll. I'd recognize those eyebrows anywhere, although he'd taken a vow of silence, and I'd had to carry the conversation."

Stewart had reached the bottom of the stairs now and waited impatiently for his pregnant wife and brother-in-law. Skye shook her head, as she stepped in front of Duncan, in order to gain his full attention.

"He is nae monk," she repeated again, slower. "Mayhap ye saw a man who looks like him?"

Duncan's frown grew as he shook his head, although he was beginning to look unconvinced. "I would swear on my life 'tis the same man."

"Mayhap 'tis Harold, but he didnae want to speak?"

She scoffed at Fergus's explanation. "*And* he wore a monk's habit? Why would he no' want to speak?"

The old man shrugged. "Because of his voice?"

Harold's voice had been ruined years before in a childhood injury to his neck, and he often only spoke to Allison during his visits.

There was a noise like a spat, but also a growl. It dragged everyone's attention away from Lady MacIan and her brother...to Pierre.

The Frenchman was staring at Harold, hatred burning intensely in his eyes, as his knuckles went white around the hilt of his sword.

"Pierre?" Skye asked hesitantly.

"*Raque Harold*," Pierre spat out. "*Il a tué mon frère. Je vous ai rejoint pour le trouver,*" he growled. "*Maintenant j'aurai ma revanche!*"

"Purple," Bean offered.

But Duncan's eyes had gone wide. "*Raque* Harold! By St. Simon's nostrils, *of course.*" He stepped toward the couple, who'd just reached the bottom of the stairs, his hand going to his own sword. "I cannae believe I didnae realize!"

Skye placed her hand on his arm, ready to do her best to wrench him back if he didn't explain what in the seven holy hells was going on. "What did ye no' realize?" she asked, struggling to keep her voice calm.

Thankfully, Duncan heard her and whirled back around, his dark eyes bright with excitement.

"*Raque* is French for 'hoarse,' Skye!"

And suddenly she understood. "Allison's brother is Hoarse Harold, the notorious highwayman?"

"*Figtart! Honied oatcake!* The man's stayed under our roof more than once," Fergus hissed, looking ready to do battle himself.

"Of course," Skye whispered; her eyes wide. "And just today, Allison mentioned to me she had to check on an order of caltrops with the MacIan blacksmith."

The noxious little weapons Hoarse Harold used had been made right here on MacIan land!

"Remember how his tarting men wore monks' habits—or were they priests?—last time we met?"

He had traveled on the road from Eriboll, and Duncan saw him. He wore a disguise and didnae speak, for fear of his voice being recognized."

The old man growled, "And then when yon goldsmith stole ye away, the custardy fruitcake and his men attacked us!"

"Aye, but ye defeated them, remember?" She placed her other hand over Fergus's, where it rested on his hilt, reminding him to stay calm. "If he *is* the reason Allison has been stealing our coin, he is here because he is desperate."

"Ye were forced to turn highwayman, my love," Duncan said, with a twinkle in his eyes, "because yon highwayman had his sister stealing MacIan coin for him."

Sure enough, Skye watched as—while Stewart's back was turned—Allison slipped her brother a pouch of something heavy.

"We cannae let him just walk away," she whispered.

Duncan half-pulled his sword from his scabbard. "We *willnae*."

She loved him, aye, but she could not allow him to be hurt over what was definitely *her* family's business. So she wrapped both of her hands around his arm and squeezed gently, then increased the pressure until he looked at her.

"Ye are nae swordsman, Duncan. Ye've said so many times."

"Och, well…" His smile was slightly lopsided. "I'm no' all that bad. Come."

And with that, he began pulling her toward the little group by the stairs.

But at least his blade remained in his scabbard, for which she was thankful.

They must've looked a sight, striding across the great hall. Duncan's legs were long, and she had to pull up her skirts with one hand to keep up—because she wasn't losing her grip on him. Fergus, Bean and Pierre trailed behind, but she was certain they all looked threatening.

Allison took a step back, her face paling, and her brother moved off to one side. When Duncan careened to a stop before him, Harold's unfortunate eyebrows shot straight up.

They look like a pair of caterpillars kissing atop his forehead.

"What's the meaning of this?" Laird Stewart MacIan spoke first, obviously determined to maintain the respect due to his rank. "Are ye Finn Oliphant, or his brother?"

Duncan was still glaring at Harold, but he growled, "His brother."

Skye flapped her hand at her brother. "This is Duncan, Stewart. I love him and plan on marrying him." Before her brother could do aught more than suck in a surprised breath, she continued with, "Now please shut yer mouth and listen to him."

Allison squeaked, "*Skye! Manners!*" but everyone ignored her.

Pointing one strong, callused finger at Allison's brother, Duncan pierced the man with a fierce look. "Ye are Hoarse Harold, the infamous highwayman, are ye no'?"

As Allison suck in another breath—had she sounded offended, or frightened?—Harold drew himself up. "I am no'."

"Aye, ye are," Duncan asserted.

"Am no'."

"Ye *are.*"

Harold waggled those remarkable eyebrows. "Prove it."

"*Je sais qui tu es,*" Pierre said in a menacing tone, as he stepped up beside Duncan, "*connard d'une chèvre enceinte, et tu paieras pour ce que tu as fait!*"

Allison's brother paled slightly and swallowed.

Does everyone around here understand French except me?

"As Hoarse Harold, you murdered Pierre's brother." Duncan's eyes gleamed with victory. "Even if we cannae prove ye are a notorious highwayman, we *can* prove ye've been stealing from the Maclans!"

Harold paled even further, and Allison made a little whimpering sound, swaying on her feet and reaching for her brother's arm. He shook her off, but neither could hide their looks of nervousness.

Stewart obviously had had enough of being left in the dark. "What is that supposed to mean?" he growled, stepping up beside his brother-in-law and glaring at Duncan. "Ye come into my home and accuse my family of crimes?"

It was time for Skye to step in.

With her eyes on Allison, she spoke to her brother. "Have ye no' noticed how much of our coin yer wife is spending, Stewart? How we're losing *all* our income to her whims?"

As Allison lowered her orange brows and glowered at Skye, Stewart glanced at his wife and shook his head. "I— She is the Lady MacIan, carrying my heir. I indulge her love of finery—"

" 'Tis more than that, Stewart, and ye *ken* it," Skye snapped. "That is a fine gown she's wearing, aye, but—"

"And ye as well!" Allison interrupted, sounding more than a little desperate. "I only want my husband's family to appear benefitting their station! And speaking of yer gown, why do ye look as if ye've been rolling in the hay?" Her smirk looked forced, as she flicked a glance at Duncan. "As if I need ask."

The bitch thought to distract everyone from the current line of questions?

Ha!

" 'Tis nae *me* we are discussing, Allison." Skye fought to keep her voice even. "The MacIan family has stood united long before ye arrived. Stewart and I have nae need for finery—never have—or for appearing grander than we really are. Ye are the one with that obsession, but even that does no' account for the amount of missing coin over the last year."

Allison swung around to face her husband, but Stewart—thank the saints—was staring at his wife with a thoughtful look.

"Stewart! *Husband!* Ye cannae believe this—this *tatterdemalion lass* over yer own wife."

When she reached for his arm, Stewart didn't react; he didn't move closer, but didn't shrug her off either. "That *lass* is my sister, and I ken she cares for this clan as much as I do."

"So ye think I...*what?*" Allison gasped. "I've been *stealing* from ye?"

"*Have* ye?"

The pregnant woman began to sway, then lifted the back of one wrist to her forehead and moaned theatrically.

"Ye can faint later, Allison. I want to ken if ye've been wasting my coin."

Skye loosened her grip on Duncan's arm and stepped up beside her brother, proudly. "She's no' just been wasting coin, brother, but funneling it to *her* brother, a highwayman. Even now, I suspect ye'll find a pouch from the MacIan coffers on his person."

Stewart's hands curled into fists as he shook off his wife's hand. "For a year, ye've sat and listened to me speak of my clan's financial woes, as a good wife would, but never once thought to speak up and tell me *where* my coin was going? Ye *stole* from me, Allison?"

Weakly, Allison stumbled toward one of the benches against the wall, her face pale, moaning Stewart's name.

And Skye smiled proudly at her brother. No matter what else came out of this confrontation, at least she knew Laird MacIan would no doubt have his wife well under control from that day forward.

Which meant she could leave the MacIans in capable hands.

Since Stewart was obviously still reeling from the revelation of his wife's betrayal, it was Duncan who shoved a finger in Harold's face. "If ye ken what is good for ye, ye'll return the pouch of MacIan coin yer sister just passed to ye!"

And Harold stepped *closer*. "Oh, I *ken* what is good for me: Exercise, leafy green vegetables, regular digestive intervals, and thrice-daily prayer. But I doubt 'tis what ye had in mind."

Duncan's hand dropped to his hilt. "Return the coin," he growled.

In one smooth motion, Harold drew his blade, stepping to the side to allow himself enough room to maneuver.

In a mocking voice, he waggled the tip at Duncan's chest. "Make me," he taunted.

Skye was already reaching for the dagger always strapped to her belt, but when Duncan ripped his own sword from the scabbard, she felt her stomach drop into her knees.

He is nae swordsman!

CHAPTER 11

DUNCAN FORCED himself to keep his breathing even as he lifted his blade to protect Skye. Harold hadn't actually threatened her, but there was no way Duncan could allow the highwayman to brandish a sword anywhere near Duncan's beloved.

"Drop yer sword," he growled. "Return the coin yer sister passed ye, and ye might be allowed to leave here alive."

He had no interest in killing Harold, although he was fairly confident in his ability to hold his own in a battle.

For years, his father and Rocque—the Oliphant commander—had trained him. And for years, Duncan had somewhat begrudgingly listened. He didn't believe there was much reason for him to know how to thrust and parry, since he planned to spend his life behind a forge, creating beautiful, delicate pieces of art.

But he'd acknowledged years ago, if the Oliphant Laird ever called his men to battle, Duncan needed to be prepared. Besides, his stepfather Edward had always said, in order to forge well-balanced weapons, a smith had to understand how to wield them as well.

And *that's* why Duncan hadn't hesitated to pull his sword and to step toward Harold—who was sneering and had a bloodthirsty look in his eyes—and stand between Skye and danger.

However, Harold didn't seem impressed.

"*I* think, instead, I'll stroll from this keep, get on my horse, and spend the coin as I like."

Stewart's sharp intake of breath told all of those present he'd heard the admission of guilt, and now, finally understood what his wife and brother-in-law were capable of.

Thank fook! Now I can marry Skye and get her away from this nonsense.

But it was Fergus who spoke up. "Have yer tarting custards recovered from the berries-and-cream whooping we gave them the last time we met?"

Harold narrowed his eyes, his attention pulled from Duncan. "*What?*"

"Yer henchmen," the old man clarified. "Ye might've been dressed as monks, but we kicked yer bloody—excuse me, *figtarty*—arses, we did!"

"I hit one on the head," Bean rumbled happily.

"*Oui! Maudits laches!*"

Duncan watched Harold's expression as the other man glanced from Fergus to Pierre to Bean, and saw the exact moment he realized these men were part of another group of highwaymen.

"*Ye're—*"

But Duncan wasn't going to allow the bastard to accuse Skye's men of banditry, not where her brother could hear anyway. With a bellow, he raised his sword and charged the other man.

Harold got his own blade up just in time to block, and the two men spun around one another. This time, Harold went on the offensive, raising his sword high over his own head, then hacking down toward Duncan's head, while Duncan did his best to deflect and turn his opponents attack against him.

Duncan drew first blood when the tip of his blade slid across the orange-haired highwayman's upper arm.

Harold fell back with a hiss, but forgot to consider his surroundings. He was facing Duncan, aye, and the others had fallen back, aye.

All but Skye, who—*St. Simon's kidney stones,* she'd pulled out her dagger?—was advancing from Harold's rear.

Duncan's blood ran cold. He was suddenly terrified Harold would turn and see Skye as a threat.

Lifting his blade again, Duncan did his best to hold the other man's attention. "Ye are outnumbered and outmatched, ye ox-brained son of a diseased pig." He couldn't attack Harold, because that would drive the man backward, toward Skye. "Come show me what ye're made of."

Mayhap the bloodying had made the highwayman cautious though, because he was breathing heavily when he lifted his own blade and stood firm. "Nay, ye bastard. Come show *me* what *ye're* made of."

How had he known Duncan was a bast—*Oh, 'twas an insult.*

"Nay, I want to ken what *ye're* made of!"

Harold snorted. "Come show me, then."

Dunc shook his head. "Nay, ye show *me*."

"I am right here. *Ye* show *me*."

'Twas getting ridiculous.

Stewart was the one who finally broke their stalemate. "Ye are my wife's brother, Harold, but if ye value the laws of hospitality, ye'll—"

None of them ever found out what the MacIan Laird intended to say, because at that moment, Skye reached Harold.

Honestly, Duncan hadn't been completely certain she wasn't going to plunge her dagger into the man's back. His Skye was wild, impetuous, and difficult to predict sometimes.

But instead, in one swift movement, she reached out, grabbed the pouch of coins dangling from the man's belt, and sliced through the leather thong.

As the heavy pouch fell into her grasp, she stepped back, at the same moment Harold realized what had happened.

He began to turn, his face turning even redder, and Skye—obviously desperate to be out of his reach—scrambled back quickly, then tripped over her gown and went sprawling on her delectable arse, leaving her completely exposed to the evil man's attack.

Duncan wasn't going to let that happen.

With a roar, he lifted his blade and charged.

The action had Harold's attention whipping back around, and he clambered to turn, trying to get his blade up to block the attack.

Pierre yelled, Fergus cursed—*"Figtart!"*—and Bean stepped forward with his fists raised menacingly.

Why in damnation did the man refuse to use a perfectly good sword?

The question flitted through Duncan's mind in the split second it took for his own blade to crash down upon Harold's.

The other man dropped his sword on impact.

Just like a lad on the first day of training. Harold *dropped* his *sword.*

Mayhap he was as embarrassed as he should've been, because with a panicked gasp, Hoarse Harold, the MacIan Laird's brother-by-marriage, turned and ran from the keep.

"Il n'ira pas loin!" Pierre hollered, rushing out after him, his blade raised. *"Renez le vagin meurtrier d'un âne malade!"*

Fergus and Bean followed him, calling out for support among the MacIan warriors. For a moment, Duncan was afraid Skye would follow. He hurried to slide his sword back into the scabbard, his hands shaking with fear over how close she'd come to harm.

By the time he reached her, Skye was pushing herself to her feet, and Duncan quickly pulled her into his arms, tucking her head under his chin. He was gratified by the way her arms snaked around his middle, and he could feel the hilt of the dagger she still carried press into his lower back.

She was shaking, but so was he.

"Shh, love. I have ye," he murmured, inhaling her leather-and-pear scent.

St. Simon's foot, he *loved* this woman!

In the moment he thought Harold might harm her, Duncan had never known such terror.

If there'd been any doubt in his mind, this incident would've alleviated it immediately.

"I love ye," she whispered against his chest.

And he thanked the saints above she was his, and was safe and sound in his arms.

Far too little time had passed before he felt her stir, and her brother cleared his throat. Reluctantly, Duncan allowed her to straighten and pull away from him, although he kept one arm around her.

With her tucked up next to his side, they both turned to Stewart, who was looking more than a little bewildered.

"Ye just challenged my brother-in-law to battle in my great hall," he murmured, raking Duncan with a confused glance. "And Skye, how did ye ken...?"

Under Duncan's arm, she shrugged and hefted the bag of coins. Seemed as if *she* wasn't going to admit her highwaywomaning to her brother willingly either.

"Allison has been stealing from us for a while, brother," was all she said.

All three of them looked at the pregnant woman, who still sat slumped on the bench. While they watched, one of her eyes peeked open, and as she saw their gazes, she hurried to moan and slam her eyes shut again.

Stewart snorted softly, then straightened his shoulders. Raising his voice, he spoke to Skye, but no one doubted his words were mostly for Allison's benefit.

"Well, I appreciate learning of this perfidy, for certes. My *wife* will have some explaining to do. She might be my people's mistress and carrying my heir, but she is accountable to *me* and God, and I can promise ye, she'll no' have any more access to MacIan coin."

From her spot beside the wall, Allison gave a pitiful little whimper, but Skye was beaming at her brother.

"Then I suppose I should return this to ye."

She lobbed him the coin purse, which he easily caught. When he opened it, Duncan could see the glint of gold from inside.

"I *will* be taking charge of the books myself from now on. This might no' restore us to where we were, but losing this much would've made things so much more difficult to recover from." He inclined his head to his sister. "Thank ye, Skye."

Skye stood a little straighter and looked up to smile at Duncan. "Dunc was the man who stopped Harold, Brother."

"Ah, aye." Stewart tucked the pouch into his belt, then shifted his weight as he crossed his arms in front of his chest. "And now, about what ye said earlier…"

Duncan was busy wracking his brain, trying to figure out what she'd said, when Skye chuckled.

"Ye mean, when I told ye I loved Duncan and plan on marrying him?"

"Aye, that part. Right before ye rudely demanded I 'shut my mouth' and listen to a *smith*." This time, the gaze he raked Duncan with was very much one from a man debating another man's worth. "Ye want to marry a *smith*, Sister?"

Before Skye could do more than bristle, Duncan bent and placed one arm behind her knees. She squealed as he lifted her into the air, but wrapped her arms around his neck.

They didn't have the time or need for this blathering. Duncan and Skye would be together, and the sooner Stewart got that through his head, the better.

Besides, he couldn't wait much longer to get her clothing off and show her *exactly* how much she meant to him.

But *first*…

He pierced her brother with a confident grin. "I'm no' just a smith, but the best *goldsmith* between Inverness and Lairg. My offer of marriage comes with a sizable enough bride price to replace most of what yer wife stole from ye." As Stewart's brows went up, Duncan nodded firmly. "So ye best get it into yer head; Skye will be my wife, with or without yer permission."

"Ye cannae just declare—"

But Duncan was already stalking toward the stairs, his love in his arms.

Behind him, Stewart called out, "Where are ye going?"

"To take off all of yer sister's clothes and kiss every inch of her," Duncan called back, without stopping.

He didn't hear The MacIan's response, because he was too busy chuckling when Skye let out an excited whoop.

"Turn right to get to my chambers!"

And the knowledge she was his, and *would be his* forever, had his cock jumping in anticipation. He increased his pace, ready to have her.

Always.

"GOD IN HEAVEN, THAT WAS *REMARKABLE*," Skye panted, as Duncan rolled off her with a groan.

They were both breathing heavily, their releases coming fast and furious, after they'd torn each other's clothing off.

"Remarkable?" he teased; his eyes closed. "*That's* the best ye can say?"

She was smiling when she propped her elbow on the bed and rolled to face him. He was nude, a thin sheen of sweat covering his chest, which still heaved from the aftereffects of their lovemaking.

" 'Twas no' bad at all, I suppose."

"*No' bad?*" He opened one eye and glared at her.

"For the first round," she clarified with a straight face. "I assume we'll get better with practice.

He groaned and threw a forearm across his eyes. "Love, if we get any *better*, I'll probably die."

The urge to tickle him was fierce, especially with how pitiful he looked, believing her words. Instead, she dragged her fingertips down his chest.

"Die?" she murmured.

"My heart will explode. Or my cock will. One of the two."

She burst into chuckles.

With a growl, he erupted into motion, grabbing her and rolling once more, so she was pinned underneath him. Their bodies were sticky from their previous exertions, and she wouldn't mind a bath later—*ooh*, a bath *with* him!—but for now, she was delighted to have him close to her again.

"Are ye *trying* to kill me, lass?"

"And make myself a widow before I'm a bride? *Never*."

The reminder sobered him, and his dark eyes caressed her face. "Ye really are willing to marry me, Skye?"

She blinked. "Of course. Ye overcame the impediments quite nicely, ye ken. Now that Allison will no' be stealing from my clan, I dinnae feel like I *have* to be here."

"And the highwaywomaning?"

He was becoming heavy, and when she squirmed underneath him, he took the hint. He pushed himself up on his elbow, and she let out a breath as she rolled as well, until she was sitting cross-legged beside him.

It was time to speak of the future.

"Ye want me to settle down. To be a wife in yer cozy little black-smith cottage. To learn to cook and sew and—"

She bit off her words with a gasp when he abruptly sat up, rolling to his heels there beside her on her bed.

Good God, but he was glorious, all naked skin and firm muscles, and who would've thought she'd have a thing for such nicely toned forearms?

…What had she been saying?

Whatever it was, it went right out of her head when he leaned to one side and swiped something off the table.

When he moved again, she realized it was the braided gold ring he'd made, and she'd worn for the last sennight. In their frantic haste to disrobe, she'd tossed it onto the table for safekeeping.

Now she watched him untie the silk ribbon which held it and drop the simple piece of jewelry into his palm.

When he took her hand and slipped the ring on her third finger, she sucked in a breath, surprised by how *warm* the gold was against her finger. Then he placed a kiss on the band.

"I love ye the way ye are, Skye MacIan," he said, in that gravelly voice she loved, while holding her gaze intently. "I love yer wild impulsiveness. I dinnae want ye to *settle*. All I'm asking is fer ye to give up yer lawbreaking. I cannae spend my life worrying for ye."

She snorted. "Worrying for *me*? I'm no' the one who attacked a known brigand today, with a sword he claims he doesnae ken how to use."

Duncan sat back, his lips twisting wryly. "I ken how to use it; I just dinnae *like* to use it. We cannae all be swordswomen, love."

"Good, because ye'd look silly in a gown." She reached out and tweaked one of his nipples.

Playfully slapping her hand down, he then trapped it against his chest. "Ye were worried for me?"

Under his skin, she could feel his heart beating strongly, and reminded herself it was beating for *her*. He was safe, and he was *hers*.

And would be forever.

"I love ye, Dunc," she whispered, holding his gaze. "I'll always worry for ye."

"Then ye ken how I felt when I saw ye sneaking up on Harold with yer dagger out. St. Simon's eyeteeth, lass, ye scared the piss out of me!"

Her eyes widened. It honestly hadn't occurred to Skye he would worry over her.

He began to chuckle. "Aye, it works both ways. If we're to be married, I'll worry for ye, the same as ye'll worry for me. And we both need to agree to do our best *no'* to worry the other. Deal?"

It was simple. "If ye mean me giving up my highwaywomaning, aye. Deal. I was only doing it for my clan, and although we're good at it, the lads will be pleased to give it up as well."

"Fergus struck me as a bit of a worrier himself."

She chuckled, and under his hand, began to move her fingers in small circles against his nipple. "Aye, he's been trying to talk me into quitting for a while now. Bean will go along with whatever we decide. Rabbie—that's Fergus's nephew—"

"The weaselly looking one?" Duncan interrupted.

The description fit.

"Aye," she agreed with a chuckle. "He's the only one who'll really miss the work, I think, but he'll be Stewart's problem once I'm gone."

"And Pierre?"

She shrugged. "Who kens why Pierre was even with us to begin with?"

When he cocked his head, she suddenly remembered Duncan spoke French.

"He said Harold killed his brother. Was it possible he joined yer band as a way to hunt him down?"

'Twas likely, but Duncan had lifted her hand away from his chest and was now tracing small circles on her palm, which was making it difficult for her to focus.

"I… Mayhap…" she murmured vaguely, her gaze dropping to where he held her hand.

The gold ring glinted enchantingly.

He lifted it to his lips, then brushed a kiss to the inside of her wrist.

Her pulse jumped, and she realized she was holding her breath.

"So we're agreed?" he murmured against her skin, brushing her fingertips across his lips. "Nae more lawbreaking for ye, and we'll navigate this marriage thing as we go along?"

Her gaze was locked on his lips.

"Aye…"

When he smiled, 'twas as if someone had tied a string to her nipples and *pulled*. She gasped, jerking forward, toward him.

And he caught her.

"Well then, mayhap we should seal our bargain with a kiss."

God help her, would that delicious deep voice of his always affect her this way?

She could feel herself growing wet for him…again!

Instinctively, her gaze dropped to his lap, and aye, that magnificent cock of his—which she'd seen long before she'd ever touched— had grown in size.

"A kiss?" she repeated.

"I told yer brother I intended to kiss every inch of ye, and 'twould be rude of me to lie to my future brother-by-marriage."

He sounded so solemn, it caused her gaze to snap back up to his. The twinkle in his dark eyes told her he was teasing, so she rallied.

"Och, well, I wouldnae kick ye out of bed," she offered with a nonchalant shrug belied by the way she was holding her breath.

That breath was knocked out of her with a chuckle when he tackled her, pushing her into the mattress, before lowering his lips to hers.

Her hand wrapped around his cock, guiding it to her aching entrance, and while she wrapped her legs around his hips and threw her head back in ecstasy, she vowed to be the best wife she could to Duncan.

Because together, they were both going to be wild and perfect.

Forever.

EPILOGUE

ANOTHER WEDDING.

Rocque Oliphant stood on the outskirts of the crowded celebration in the village square, and reflected on how the festivity wasn't so different from Finn's recent wedding.

St. John's thumbs, even the bride and groom *looked* the same, what with Duncan and Skye being identical to Finn and Fiona.

But no one could confuse the couples. While Finn and Fiona had celebrated their marriage in the castle, and even now wore their fine silks, Dunc and Skye had chosen to celebrate among the clan.

Hard to blame them. The Oliphants ken how to throw a revel.

Of course, Duncan had likely made the choice so his other family —his mam's family—would feel comfortable celebrating with them. As Rocque watched, Dunc grabbed one of his two younger sisters and swung her around, as wee Ned bowed low in front of Skye.

And Rocque ignored the spike of jealousy, which slid down his tongue and into his belly.

Just as he'd been ignoring it for years.

"Ye're just going to stand here, glaring at everyone?"

The snappish voice jerked him from his thoughts, and he was already shaking his head as he turned to find his great-aunt on Kiergan's arm.

"I'm no' glaring, Aunt Agatha. Just admiring how much fun everyone's having."

Her cane slammed against his shin, and Rocque schooled his features from letting her see how much it had hurt.

"Ye disagree?" he asked her smartly.

As his aunt clucked her tongue, Kiergan came to his defense. "He's likely just watching his new men, Aunt. Ye see how Bean—'tis the giant's name—is laughing with Rocque's warriors. I ken 'twas odd Skye brought the three men with her, but they seem to be fitting in well enough."

"I *see* how the lad's head is even thicker than Rocque's here—"

"Thank ye, Aunt Agatha," Rocque murmured, used to the jibes.

"—but 'tis that handsome aulder man—Fergus, I think his name is?—I cannae ignore. He has a nice smile, do ye no' think?" Before either of her great nephews could do more than gape at her in shock, she continued. "That Frenchman now, I dinnae trust him. Look at the way he flirts with yer sister!"

Kiergan didn't seem concerned. "She doesnae understand anything he says—none of us do—and Da's already signed her betrothal contract."

"Again."

Rocque grunted in rare agreement with his great-aunt. Poor Nessa had lost three—although it was hard to keep count—betrotheds already. Da was determined to get her wed.

The old woman clucked her tongue again. "If she's been hearing the drummer, yer father will have naught to say in it!"

"*This* again?" Kiergan groaned under his breath.

The ghostly drummer of Oliphant Castle was famous. Not everyone heard him, but those who did, were said to be destined for love. Kiergan didn't believe in the legend.

Rocque wasn't certain how he felt about the legend himself, but he'd been hearing the cursed annoying bastard for the last year.

Since Kiergan had helped him, Rocque distracted his aunt's attention in return, since she was clearly about to start in on his poor brother.

"I *was* watching the men. I'm glad Dunc decided to have his wedding here, where everyone could participate." As the Oliphant commander, he took his duties—which included keeping an eye on his men—seriously. "And I was thinking how happy the bride and groom look together."

There. None of that was a lie.

"Aye," Kiergan was quick to latch on to the change in subject. " 'Tis as I told ye, Aunt Agatha. He wasnae glaring; he was examining the revelry for signs of weakness. In case any enemies attack."

"Bah! Who would attack us on a summer afternoon? The lad was glaring."

Rocque felt his lips twitch at the old woman's feistiness. "Thank ye so much for bringing Aunt Agatha over to say hello, Kiergan."

His brother dipped his head, as if he hadn't heard the sarcasm. "The pleasure was all mine."

"I'm right here, ye clot-heids!" Before either of them could apologize for speaking about her as if she weren't present, she slammed the end of her cane down against the ground. "Ye two will be next, I assume? Dragging yer true loves in front of a priest?"

Kiergan snorted, but that was to be expected. When Da had made the announcement he expected them all to marry, this rakish brother of theirs had been the only one to outright refuse.

But since he'd spoken up for Rocque, the larger man was willing to return the favor. "*I've* considered it, Aunt," he said mildly, knowing it would pull her attention away from his brother.

Sure enough, her sharp gaze swung to him like a hawk…if the hawk were four and a half feet tall and armed with an oaken cane.

"Ye've considered marriage?" she repeated, her intense stare a little unnerving.

He shrugged, his gaze darting to Kiergan's, looking for help. "Aye, well, Da says we must, and…" He shrugged again.

Just as Aunt Agatha opened her mouth—likely to question him further—Kiergan spoke up. "Och, look! Lara finally dragged her brother away from Bean. Let us go greet them."

The interruption pushed Aunt Agatha off-balance, and she swung her gaze around to Kiergan. "What?"

"Lara," he repeated unhelpfully, jerking his chin across the square. "Over there. *Way* over there. Come along."

Dragging their protesting aunt through the revelers, Kiergan threw a wink over his shoulder at Rocque, who vowed to go easy on this brother of his, next time he was called up for guard duty.

The square was still a riot of colors and noise as the revelers celebrated, but without Aunt Agatha at his side, Rocque felt able to relax.

Relax...and consider her words.

Would he be next to marry?

Da had said they all had to marry, and the appeal of leadership was hard to deny. True, Rocque knew he wasn't the smartest of the Oliphant bastards—that title belonged to his twin—but he'd been leading the clan's men for a few years now and was no stranger to leadership.

Did he *want* to be the next laird?

If ye do, ye best get moving.

In order to become laird, he'd have to present his father with a legitimate grandson. In order to sire a legitimate grandson, he needed a wife.

And how hard could it be to get a wife?

No' just any wife, laddie.

He sighed.

Nay, if he were honest with himself, no' just any woman would do.

There was only one woman who filled his thoughts...and his nights. Only one woman who made him smile and considered his needs.

Only one woman he *wanted* to marry.

As if his thoughts had conjured her, a pair of small, lightly callused hands slipped in front of his eyes. "Guess who?"

He didn't need to guess; Rocque's lips curled upward.

She was the only woman he knew who carried the smell of herbs around with her. If that weren't enough of a hint—if his nose were plugged or some such thing—then the feel of her breasts pushing against his back as she held her hands over his eyes, would be more than enough.

He knew those breasts. He knew that body.

He knew this woman.

Still smiling, he turned in her arms, pulling her even closer. "Hello, Merewyn."

Her arms snaked around his neck, and he settled his big hands on her hips, snugging her up against his hardening cock.

"Hello, lover," she said with an impish smile, as she tugged his lips down to hers.

This kiss was quick, but hot enough to make Rocque long for the quiet of her little cottage. He pulled back and placed his forehead against hers, loving the feel of her in his arms.

"Marry me, Mere."

When she sucked in a gasp, he straightened, wanting to be looking into her eyes when she agreed to become his wife.

The look in her eyes faded from shock to…to something else, as her fingers still played in the hair at the base of his neck. She didn't say anything for a long time, and he began to wonder if she was doubting his proposal.

"Merewyn, we fit well enough. Marry me. Be my wife."

"Oh, Rocque," she said softly, her lips curling into a soft sort of smile. " 'Tis sweet of ye to ask."

So why wasn't she agreeing?

"Ye will, aye?"

She shook her head, her gaze turning apologetic. "Nay. I cannae marry ye."

AUTHOR'S NOTE

AUTHOR'S NOTE
   on Historical Accuracy

There's no historical accuracy.
   There. Boom. Author's Note done.

Ha, but seriously. There's no year indicated in this series (on purpose), and the locations are vague, at best. Again, on purpose. I seriously hope you didn't pick up this book—or this series—expecting it to be historically accurate?

I set out to write a comedy as near to something Shakespeare might write—complete with dick and fart jokes—as possible. I think I nailed it, but maybe that's because I have an immature sense of humor.

Seriously, the only thing I can think to mention is that Lairg and Larg are the same place (Larg is the historic spelling of the current town). And that there were plenty of Frenchmen (and women!) gallivanting around Scotland during its long history...thanks mainly to the treaties between the two countries.

I should also point out that my editor gave me grief about not translating all of Pierre's lines. But if you went through the effort of translating them, then you know that was the point. If you *didn't*... well, then, you're missing half the jokes!

Um...yep. That's it. Nothing else about this book was serious enough to warrant an Author's Note! We're done!

Anyhow, I'd love to know what you think of the *Hots for Scots* series. Find me on Facebook or email me at Caroline@CarolineLeeRomance.com and let me know!

If you enjoyed the book, and are curious about the rest of the Oliphant lads, you're in luck; Rocque's story is ready for you! He's fallen for a woman who is as hard-headed as he is! Keep reading for a sneak peek at *Getting Scot and Bothered!*

But first, I want to offer you a personal invitation to my reader group. If you're on Facebook, I hope you'll consider joining. It's where I post all the best book news first, and you'll be able to get to know me personally. My Cohort is also instrumental in helping me name characters and choose covers! So stop on by!

And now, for Rocque and his Merewyn...

SNEAK PEEK

Wow. When Rocque worked up the bollocks to offer marriage to Merewyn, the Oliphant healer, she just flat-out turned him down, huh? Don't tell me you're not curious what's going on with *that* relationship!

Well, wonder no more, my friends, because Rocque and Merewyn are waiting for you in *Getting Scot and Bothered!*

He loved waking up beside her.

There was something about waking up in a woman's bed; knowing the sheets were all clean and fresh-smelling, and there'd be something warm to break his fast. But 'twas not just *any* woman who made him smile when he opened his eyes.

'Twas Merewyn.

Grinning, he rolled over and propped himself up on his elbow. She was stretched out beside him, limbs akimbo, the coverlet kicked down around her waist and one of her red curls stuck in the dried drool beside her mouth. As he watched, she grunted and shifted position, as if personally affronted by the pillow.

She was beautiful.

He loved the way she could be as stubborn as he was, unwilling to settle for anything less than what she knew was the best. And as the Oliphant healer, Merewyn *often* knew what was best.

For everyone else, at least.

Rocque's smile slowly faded as he remembered the night before. They'd made love, and he'd asked—yet again—for her hand in marriage.

And yet again, she turned him down.

Gently, he placed his large hand against her stomach, and when she didn't move, spread his fingers across her skin. He could imagine her swelling with his bairns, caring for them the way she cared for the villagers. They could be *happy* here together, in this little cottage.

She murmured something, and his gaze darted up to her face, but her eyes were still closed. And his lips twitched upward once more.

He'd been with her for almost a year. They'd spent the long winter keeping one another warm here in this very bed. He knew what she liked, and knew she liked what *he* liked.

Like mutual morning *likings*, for one thing.

Slowly, sneakily, he shifted until he was lying beside her, his body stretched out along hers, and his manhood already aching. She smelled of rosemary—the way she always did.

'Twas his favorite scent.

Mayhap the movement woke her, because she rolled toward him and opened her eyes.

They laid like that, their heads sharing the same pillow, gazing at one another.

He knew the moment she blinked away all the sleep, the moment she realized his unspoken suggestion.

Her brow twitched. "Good morning, lover."

He lifted himself up on one elbow, looming over her, and her lips stretched lazily to match his. As he lowered his lips, she reached one arm up to pull him closer.

A good morning, indeed.

Oh boy! This book is going to be *hot*! Check our Rocque and Merewyn's contentious affair in *Getting Scot and Bothered!*

ABOUT THE AUTHOR

Caroline Lee has been reading romance for so long that her fourth-grade teacher used to make her cover her books with paper jackets. But it wasn't until she (mostly) grew up that she realized she could *write* it too. So she did.

Caroline is living her own little Happily Ever After in NC with her husband, sons, and brand-new daughter, Princess Wiggles. And while she doesn't so much "suffer" from Pittakionophobia as think that all you people who enjoy touching Band-Aids and stickers are the real weirdos, she *does* adore rodents, and never met a wine she didn't like. Caroline was named Time Magazine's Person of the Year in 2006 (just like everyone else) and is really quite funny in person. Promise.

You can find her at www.CarolineLeeRomance.com.

Printed in Great Britain
by Amazon

45002850R00086